REVIEWS FOR
DECEIVED: A SAM MCCLELLAN TALE

Finally, America Has a Comparable P.D. James!

I have read more than 400 murder mysteries and the majority were mostly average. It is rare to come across an author who devotes great skill in describing a scene so well that you can envelope yourself into the writing and be taken along with the rest. P.D. James is a master, and I think we now have an American P.D. James with Laura S. Wharton! I can smell the beaches, see the beautiful boats and feel the warmth of the sun. I cannot wait for *Stung!* (The next Sam McClellan novel)!

— **Anne-Marie Taylor**

Ultimately…Terrifying in Its Implacability!

This book was wonderful, absolutely fantastic! I adored it! I went into this book thinking "Oh, this seems like it will be a nice story." And, wow, did *Deceived* exceed my expectations and blow me away. This smartly written, thought-provoking novel is a must read for any fan of fiction.

— **James Hill**

Seriously Great Entertainment

I love Laura Wharton's character, Sam McClellan. He just seems like an all-around good guy, lives near a beach, and he's smart, too. This was my first book by her, but it won't be my last. The book started off with a bang, literally (Sam's partner, while sitting in the cop car, was shot while Sam was inside a convenience store) and led me through a multitude of suspects, good cops, bad cops, and just plain nice strangers. It was seriously fast-paced, and sometimes, I had to read things twice because my adrenaline was going so fast that my brain couldn't keep up. This was seriously great entertainment, and I highly recommend it to anyone who likes fast-paced mysteries.

— **Debbie Krenzer**

Wild Memorable Ride

I was drawn to Laura S. Wharton's book when I was looking for a nautical summer read. After forty years on the water, we're finally boatless, so I needed a fix. The author didn't let me down. The backdrop of the marinas and coves of the Intracoastal Waterway in North Carolina was so ever-present that I could smell the salt grass and fried seafood while I turned the pages. The action sequences aboard were handled with solid expertise, to the point where this old salt stopped noticing and allowed himself to become immersed in the world of the characters. Local police officer Sam McClellan is a really engaging "boatyard" kind of guy who is struggling with survivor guilt and his loyalty to his recently murdered partner. There is something seriously evil casting an ever-widening net, but Sam seems to be adrift until help arrives in the form of a quirky female hitchhiker. Unlikely partners, she and Sam enter a twisting, shadowy world of drug mules and self-anointed kingpins. Even his assumed loyal fellow police officers are not really there for him. Author Wharton takes the reader on a wild, memorable ride through all kinds of oddball scenarios, and the players uncovered at the end make the trip worthwhile. If you're looking for a well-paced summer mystery read with seagulls' cries and rum drinks, pick up a copy today. I'll be looking forward to the next book in the series.

— **Richard Sutton**

Fast-Paced and Excellent North Carolina Read

This was a really great read! The story and characters are engaging, and it moves pretty fast right from the beginning. The descriptions of the towns, waterways, and beaches of North Carolina are very accurate, and if you know the area, resonate with familiarity and are accurate and described with affection. I went ahead and ordered another book from the author but am looking forward to the next one in this series.

— **Amazon Customer**

Deceived in More Ways Than One

Life can be unpredictable. When stopping at a small convenience store, Detective Sam McClellan and his partner, Lee, never expect the end result. A bag of Fritos would cost Lee his life as someone decided to take a shot at Lee while in Sam's car. Imagine seeing your best friend and partner blown to pieces and having to deal with more than just the fallout. Finding his way back to his home, a houseboat, Sam finds himself facing even more destruction. Someone has targeted him, but why? Someone has ransacked his boat, leaving him to wonder what he or she were looking for and what he might know that would cause this to happen. But although some would think that this is a drive-by shooting and a case of being in the wrong place at the wrong time, deceptions will be revealed, lies uncovered in a small and quiet town where a strong undercurrent is about to rise, and deep secrets will come to the surface. Drugs, prostitution, betrayals, cover-ups, and distrust are just some of what author Laura Wharton uncovers for readers in one of her many mysteries: *Deceived.*

— **Fran Lewis, *New York* Reviewer**

Had a Hard Time Putting It Down

I love a good mystery. *Deceived* didn't disappoint. Right away, we learn of Officer Sam McClellan's partner and friend Lee's murder. After this, Sam's world is turned upside down. Sam is suspended and named a suspect in the murder, which sets Sam on a mission to find the killer. Sam finds deceit and lies around every corner. Bad cops, drug trafficking, murder. Whom can Sam trust? The investigation goes further than expected; many lives are in danger. As Sam and a new friend, Molly, delve into the drug-trafficking scene, they discover they have more in common than they ever thought possible. Molly's brother's murder may be connected to Lee's. Together, they will uncover the truth. Then maybe uncover a little more of each other. This book was a very good read; I had a hard time putting it down. If you like a good mystery, you should enjoy this one.

— **Amy Bartley,** *Good Reads* **Reviewer**

A Good Old-Fashioned Mystery

I love a good old-fashioned mystery and this book is just that. The author writes a fast-paced and interesting story with the perfect blend of mystery and character personality.

— **Carol Custer**

Looking Forward to the Next Sam McClellan Tale!

As a cruiser and part-time live-aboard, I believe that if we met Sam in a marina during our travels, we would enjoy sharing a cocktail with him and listening to him share his adventures! I love Wharton's books; each one I tend to read in just a day or two since I can't seem to put it down. She pays close attention to detail and keeps the suspense coming. I look forward to the next *Sam McClellan Tale*!

— **Susan McCoy**

New Series Features Crime-Solving Cop and Power-Boating Female Sidekick

Officer Sam McClellan and his partner, Lee, have stopped at a convenience store, and Sam has gone inside to buy a bag of Fritos. Meanwhile, a drive-by shooter kills Lee in

Sam's car. But what first appears to be a random act of crime soon reveals itself to be a huge cover-up of dirty secrets, drugs, prostitution, and backstabbing friends in award-winning author Laura Wharton's new novel, *Deceived,* the first novel in a new series featuring Sam McClellan. Besides its plot's many twists and turns, the novel is filled with a mix of humorous and devious characters, a touch of romance, and a pleasantly descriptive local setting along the coast of North Carolina with its many beach communities. Wharton, who has also written the coastal North Carolina novels *The Pirate's Bastard* and *Leaving Lukens,* is obviously a fan of sailing because she deftly weaves her boating passion and marine knowledge into this complex tale of intrigue, betrayal, and high stakes adventure on the open water. Nor is Wharton new to the mystery genre. She is the author of the *Lily McGuire Mystery* series and coauthor, along with her son Will Wharton, of the popular children's *Mystery at the Lake House* series. Wharton provides enough drama and action to keep her readers riveted to their seats, both fearing for the main characters and cheering them on, while also trying to guess who is a criminal and who a friend.

— **Tyler R. Tichelaar, Award-Winning Author**

What a Fun Read! I Am Familiar with the Beach Towns…
What a fun read! I am familiar with the beach towns represented in this mystery–what a nice treat to be able to picture this story taking place in locations that I know. Can't wait for the next installment of the adventures of Sam and to see what's in store for his relationship with Molly.

— **Linda Proctor, North Carolina Reader**

A Fun Read!

This is a fun read! Living on Carolina Beach and spending loads of time in Wilmington and Leland, it's neat to read the descriptors as accurately as portrayed. Can't wait to see what fun, I mean trouble, Sam and Molly get into in *Stung!*

— **Nancy Clemons, North Carolina Reader**

Excellent Read

Hard to put it down!

— **Kathy A Foster**

Get your own copy here: www.LauraWhartonBooks.com

.

STUNG!

A Sam McClellan Tale

Laura S. Wharton

LAURA S. WHARTON

First Edition: May 2016
Printed in the United States of America

Wharton, Laura S.
Stung by Laura S. Wharton
Mt. Airy, NC: Broad Creek Press, 2016
813.54
p. cm – (Stung)

Summary: Former Police Detective Sam McClellan and his mechanically-inclined, curse-spewing sassy sidekick, Molly Monroe, set out to prove Sam's Aunt Lou is not the murderer of her next-door neighbor/fiancé who died mysteriously in the pretty little North Carolina town of Edenton.

978-0-9904662-6-0 Stung (Print)
978-0-9904662-7-7 Stung (e-book)

Mystery—Fiction. 2. Beekeeping—Fiction. 3. Sailing—Fiction.
4. North Carolina—Fiction.

Visit www.LauraWhartonBooks.com.

Other Novels By
LAURA S. WHARTON

Award-winning Novels for Adults:

Deceived: A Sam McClellan Tale
In Julia's Garden, A Lily McGuire Mystery

**Award-winning Novels Suitable for
Young Adults as well as Adults:**

The Pirate's Bastard
Leaving Lukens

Award-winning Mysteries for Children:

Mystery at the Lake House #1: Monsters Below
Mystery at the Lake House #2: The Mermaid's Tale
Mystery at the Lake House #3: The Secret of the Compass
Mystery at the Phoenix Festival
The Wizard's Quest (Early Reader)

All titles are available as print and e-books.

To learn more about Laura's other books,
visit www.LauraWhartonBooks.com

TO CLAUDIA AND BOBO BRATHE:

Thanks for the porch talks.

CHAPTER ONE

"I swear I'm gonna kill you!"

Sam McClellan waved his arms ferociously toward the offender. He looked around for something to throw, but thought better of it as he quickly calculated the ensuing damage that might come if he hurled the closest wench handle at the female in his galley this morning.

This particular female was a mallard who clearly felt compelled to be Sam's first mate as he sometimes sailed, sometimes motored, his thirty-six-foot Morgan Out Island ketch up the Intercoastal Waterway toward Norfolk, Virginia. He called the mallard Kathy because she reminded Sam of a pesky past girlfriend who just wouldn't take the hint when Sam deemed the relationship over and tried repeatedly to get rid of her. This particular Kathy thought nothing of littering the boat's aft deck daily, giving the boating term "poop deck" new meaning.

On this white-hot morning, Kathy raised Sam's ire further when she waddled down the companionway stairs and made a nest in the pot of last night's leftover spaghetti noodles. Sam watched helplessly from the helm, unable to leave the wheel unattended in the Intracoastal Waterway's narrow canal, the thin spit of water known as the Alligator River-Pungo River Canal that ran north from Belhaven to the Alligator River.

Sighing, Sam checked the depth meter again. While the canal wasn't much wider than two boat-widths, it was deep—at least in the center of the canal. When a northbound power boater overtook him, Sam pushed his way to the port side of the canal where the water was uncomfortably thin. The unthinking power boater waked Sam as he throttled past, and Sam said a silent curse over the roar of his own engine.

Lined with spindly trees, this canal knew no wind. And without wind, all sailors were forced to use their "iron jennies" to make way. Sam preferred the quiet of sailing, and being waked by yet another big cruiser this morning didn't help change his perception that all power boaters were ego-driven bastards. Well, all but one.

Sam had plenty of time to think about that one person along his journey north. He also had plenty of company. Since Sam had left Carolina Beach in late August, he'd had few companions heading north. Anchoring at night was a different story. South-bound boaters were heading south, and all needed to stop just as he did at the end of the day.

Coves were filled to capacity with boats of every description and size. Sitting in his cockpit after a simple supper one evening, Sam felt envious as he watched the boaters who traveled by day in packs now party together at night, just a short row away from him. Sam marveled at the mix of partiers aboard one particularly spectacular, well-tended Island Packet. The gray-haired sailor/owner and his equally gray-haired female companion welcomed young and wizened sailors and power boaters alike, without discrimination. Sam heard their laughter float on the air late into the night. Last night, it was the hand-plucked music floating across the water between him and this boat that lulled him to sleep.

For a moment, Sam wondered whether he should pick up an instrument and learn to play since now he had time, all the time in the world, while on his long-anticipated cruise. Reaching for sunglasses hanging on a hook just inside the aft cabin, he debated what he thought might be the merits of various instruments that could be carried aboard.

Looking again at Kathy in the spaghetti pot, Sam devilishly estimated how long it would take him to turn on the propane burner under her and return to the helm without the boat steering herself into the muddy side of the channel. Sam resigned himself to waiting her out—unless she did something worse this morning. It would be a four-hour stretch before he could leave the helm, so he grabbed another bottle of water from the roughly homemade cooler under the cockpit seat.

Sam plopped down. He'd have to deal with Kathy later. To occupy his mind on the eighteen nautical-mile passage, Sam counted turtles basking on half-sunken logs that lined the banks and paid attention to the backs of the boats that passed him: *Crabby Waters, Fishel Bznus*, and *Fishin' Frenzy*. Lots of boats named *Tranquility, Destiny*, and *Solace*, or some variation thereof, passed by as well. There really wasn't much else he could do since he was traveling alone.

If he'd brought someone along, he could rest or read or shoo Kathy from her perch. If he'd brought someone along, he might get invited to attend a pack party in an anchorage some night. If he'd brought someone along…. But she wouldn't come. And Sam couldn't stay in Carolina Beach. So he traveled north to Norfolk to see his son and enjoy a taste of cruising, which he'd longed for all these years as a Carolina Beach cop. Since he shed that moniker, he was free to explore this lifestyle he'd dreamed about for years. At least until the money ran out.

Four hours later, Sam blew a relieved whistle as he left the narrow canal of the ICW and entered the wider Alligator River. Dense cypress trees lined the undeveloped swampy banks of the wide river. Now he could unfurl *Angel's* sails and shut off the engine for a few hours.

After a good afternoon's sail on the Alligator River, Sam checked his chart for anchorages. Pleased with his new spiral-bound chart book of the ICW, this was new water to

Sam. Some marinas and boat "put-in" ramps were printed on the chart's pages. Few anchorages were. Using a waterproof marker, Sam carefully drew anchors on the chart whenever he passed an entrance to a back bay for future reference. He also read short passages from a cruising guide by prolific author and avid boater Claiborne Young, a man whose books offered recommendations for stops and navigational data to readers traveling the same waters he loved. Sam appreciated Mr. Young's thoroughness, and he mentally checked off the sights he saw that were reported in the book's pages.

Spanning the river ahead of him was the aptly named Alligator River Bridge. As Sam approached the fairway, he checked his watch: approaching five o'clock. Similar swing bridges opened on the hour for recreational vessels. The Alligator River Bridge was one of the few remaining swing bridges of its kind in the state, and Sam wondered how much longer it would be before it was replaced by the high-rise monsters that spanned the waterway.

"Alligator River Bridge, Alligator River Bridge; this is the northbound sailing vessel *Angel*. What's your planned opening time? Over."

"Oh, about now," a lulling voice hissed and cracked through Sam's radio receiver. "We open on demand."

Sam watched as black and white striped barrier arms mechanically lowered in front of a few cars on either side of the bridge. Unlike many of the high-rising bridges he'd seen on his trip north, this mass of wooden slats, thick beams, and cables slowly swung open wide in a horizontal motion. When it stopped moving, Sam motored through. He offered a quick salute to the man he assumed was the bridge tender, a pipe-sucking man in coveralls leaning on the bridge railing beside the bridge house. Though the passage between the pilings was narrow, southbound motorboats flew through, waking Sam and getting a cursing from the bridge tender.

Looking ahead two hundred yards, Sam could see where the neck of the Alligator River was swallowed by a small inland ocean. He couldn't see the other side from his vantage point in the cockpit, but he knew from the chart this was the Albemarle Sound. Though Sam wasn't tired, he noted the time and decided to find an anchorage so as not to be caught on the Sound at night. Mr. Young strongly advised that this huge body of water was not one to be taken lightly. It looked placid enough, but Sam decided to take the expert author at his word. Sam chose an anchorage just at the tip of the Alligator River's eastern shore, before rounding the bend into the Albemarle Sound. The Alligator River Marina looked like a safe harbor, with fuel, a small restaurant and a ship store, and showers. While it looked like a great place to stay overnight, Sam's wallet indicated that anchoring was the way he'd go for the duration of his cruise.

As he passed the Alligator River Marina on the westerly shore, he took a quick fuel check. All of the morning's motoring had him a little nervous, but he still had enough fuel to get him well past the mouth of the Albemarle Sound and into Elizabeth City.

Approaching the head of Albemarle Sound into the face of a fierce westerly wind, Sam realized Mr. Young wasn't kidding. The wind had been mild on the Alligator River by comparison. Sam pointed *Angel* toward the eastern shore of Alligator River toward East and South Lakes at the flashing day beacon #10. Mirroring each other in shape and nearly in size, the two lakes couldn't be more different from each other, according to Mr. Young. East Lake, he reported, was shallow and chock-full of weeds eager to foul a prop. South Lake was well marked on Sam's chart, so he chose that for his anchorage.

Once inside the outer lips of the lake, Sam slowly picked his way into the second cove, a small indention on the northeastern bank. There he found six feet of water with sufficient swinging room for his thirty-six-footer. Anchoring without fuss, Sam cut his engine and marveled in the peace and beauty of the undeveloped shoreline.

Far removed from the trappings and amenities of the coastal town of Carolina Beach he'd come from, Sam would have to make do with whatever he could find to eat on board. He rummaged for food in his refrigerator with one hand and shooed Kathy out of her roost with the other. As often as he had tried to hurl her off his boat, she always found her way back to roost on his aft railing by night. Perhaps tonight she'd find a friend and leave him alone for good. Sam cleaned up Kathy's mess and the spaghetti pot.

"I'll have to stop soon for stuff," he said to no one in particular as he stirred the last of the eggs with the last inch of cheese he had. The bread was moldy, and there wasn't any fresh fruit on board. Worst of all, there wasn't any beer left. Never having cruised before, Sam had no idea how to provision properly. He was learning quickly.

Sitting on deck after cleaning the galley, Sam read more about the Albemarle Sound, a sometimes mirror-calm, sometimes raging bay whose waters deceived many a boater. Its history was full of tales of pirates, cannons lost and found, and slave traders, many of whom had vast plantations in Edenton.

Kathy preened herself on the aft rail, fresh from a swim. Watching her polish off a dinner of whatever small fish she'd found, Sam imagined hers was probably better than what he had. Tired of raging at her, Sam talked to her instead, hoping he could bore her into leaving.

"Wonder how Aunt Lou is. Wonder if she's still alive." Sam remembered visiting with his great-aunt when he was a child, and being spoiled by the then lovely, unmarried lady. He remembered she lived on a tree-lined street in a grand home that doubled as an income-producing bed-and-breakfast inn. He didn't remember much else. It had been over thirty years since he'd seen her, since she and his father had had a falling out that Sam didn't understand. Once that happened, his family never visited her again, and she didn't come to Raleigh when his family relocated from Maryland.

Sam checked his chart. "A day's sail from here. Maybe I should go visit her. I'll just zip in, say hello, and zip on to Norfolk. Besides, I sure could use some more provisions… and beer."

Without companion boaters in the anchorage or a companion on his journey, Sam read in the waning daylight. Undisturbed nature brought forth its nighttime cacophony, replete with hungry mosquitoes that chased Sam below too soon for his own taste. After a little more reading and a last check of the chart, Sam bedded down for the night. For a long time, he listened to Kathy happily quacking and snapping at mosquitoes. Decimating the mosquito population on his boat was a good thing. It was the least she could do, he thought, as he drifted off to sleep.

CHAPTER TWO

Sunbeams through the aft ports woke Sam sooner than he preferred. Try as he might, he couldn't sleep through the increasing sunlight, or the gentle rocking of *Angel*. A freshening breeze shooed remnant mosquitoes away in the early morning light, so Sam enjoyed two cups of strong black coffee in the cockpit.

With the boat as ship-shape as it would probably ever be, Sam pulled up the anchor and motored slowly out of the small cove, through the larger round lake, and into the tip of the Albemarle Sound. He hoped to leave Kathy behind during her morning swim, but she managed to land on *her* perch near the aft-mounted grill yet again this morning.

Checking the weather report on his hand-held radio, Sam pointed *Angel* toward Edenton and raised her sails, starting with the mizzen and then the main. Safely seated in the cockpit, he unfurled the jib.

As Mechanical Mike reported on the radio, a strong easterly wind filled *Angel*'s sails in a hurry. Sam steered her toward the well-marked channel of the Sound. If the wind held, he'd be in Edenton in no time.

At its widest place where it intersects the ICW, the Albemarle Sound was less than twelve nautical miles across. According to the guidebook, though, those twelve nautical miles could be turbulent and hazardous, so Sam stayed alert. Lining the sides of this freshwater inland ocean were cypress and hardwood trees, and Sam could see hints of farmland as he moved further west where the sound narrowed. He noted several rivers entering the sound, confirming with Mr. Young's book that there were nine bodies of fresh water feeding it. Unlike waters near New Bern and Oriental, there were no crab pots to dodge here in the fresh waters of the Sound. There were plenty of small fishing boats tucked into nooks and coves, making Sam sorry he never took up the pastime. It wasn't hard to imagine a life carved from the watery region's resources, and Sam reveled in the relative quiet of sailing in the brisk wind down the sound. Sam could easily see how a howling wind would make this shoal-free water so dangerous, the narrow shores funneling winds and whipping the water into an unmanageable frenzy. He was glad today was fair and fine for sailing.

By the time Sam reached the high bridge spanning the Albemarle Sound, his stomach was growling. Dashing below for a second, Sam let *Angel* self-steer so he could find the Graham crackers stashed in the back of the port settee's lazarette and grab a bottle of water. He was disappointed that these were the last of his provisions, but relieved at the same time that Edenton was just a short sail from here.

The shoreline was dotted with mansions as he rounded the last stretch of the Sound and picked up the channel markers leading into Albemarle Bay. Jutting out a little ways from the waterfront was an *L-shaped* dock dotted with tower-like electrical hookups. A town dock. Perfect.

Sam turned the key in the ignition, and *Angel's* motor roared to life. Turning the boat around to point her into the wind, Sam furled the jib, then moved forward to lower the mainsail. *Angel* made little way in the wind, and Sam could feel her bucking a bit. While he moved aft to take the mizzen down, the motor revved, whined, and died. Sam raised the mizzen again and let the wind push *Angel* back toward town. It had been a long time since he had to dock under sail, and Sam wasn't sure he wanted to try it here. From the cockpit, he checked the fuel tank located in the cockpit locker with a yardstick-turned-fuel gauge. That wasn't the problem. He unfurled the jib again and checked the chart for safe anchorage depths. Running under sail directly toward the attractive town dock, Sam made a fast dogleg left to port and ran beside the dock. He was sailing too fast to stop here, so he sailed toward a narrow channel protected from the wind by tall cypress and hardwood trees. Ahead, he could see the day markers on the fairway that could lead him to the bigger Edenton Marina. Just outside the fairway on the northeastern side was a cove, according to the chart, perfect for anchoring. Sam spilled the wind from his jib to slow his progress, and glided toward the cove. It was directly opposite the entrance to the marina, which could come in handy.

Angel's depth sounder screamed a few times, then was silent as Sam found a depth of six feet, suitable for the boat's deep keel.

Dropping his fifty-five-pound CQR anchor into the murky water, Sam tried the engine one more time to back down on the anchor rode. It wouldn't even turn over. If he had scuba gear, Sam could dive on the anchor to be sure it was secure. Since that wasn't an option, and the engine wasn't cooperating, Sam would have to pull the boat back the old-fashioned way: he'd kedge.

Lowering his dinghy into the water under Kathy's scrutiny, Sam mounted a small outboard two-stroke engine on the back of the dinghy, and he attached sturdy lines to *Angel* at the base of the boom through a metal ring on the dinghy's bow. When the weight of *Angel* turned the dinghy around, Sam cranked that engine, thankful that it started. Sam motored the dinghy slowly until the lines attached to *Angel* were taut. He pulled a little more, and when he felt *Angel* budge no more, he was comfortable in shutting down the dinghy engine and climbing aboard *Angel* to shut off the electronics. Without the ability to recharge the batteries with the engine, the electronics—including the refrigerator—would run down quickly. "Since the refrigerator is empty, that won't be a problem," Sam snickered. But having a dead engine meant there was a project, and not one that Sam relished doing at anchor.

Removing the companionway stairs, Sam got into the engine room. He checked the obvious spoil-sports: the oil, raw water intake, the belts. They were all due for replacements soon, but Sam couldn't see them as the culprit. Sam knew the diesel engine was old, though it wasn't original to the 1973 boat. *Angel's* former owner had replaced the original gasoline engine for the more fuel-efficient diesel about ten years before Sam and his then-wife purchased the boat. At the time of transferring ownership, the seller said he'd taken good care of the engine. He'd also put a lot of miles on it, using the boat primarily as a motorboat rather than what she was designed for. Now the engine was starting to show signs of sitting too long at anchor, thanks to Sam's live-aboard lifestyle in a Carolina Beach marina that only allowed for occasional day sails.

Since the electronics were still able to run, it wasn't the electrical system. It had to be the fuel system.

The injectors looked fine, and there were no signs of distress on the metal injector lines. Sam opened the throttle, then traced the throttle cable from the cockpit to the engine without finding any sticking points. Next, he bled the lines in search of air bubbles that could stop the engine cold, but no luck there, either. After he cleaned up drops of fuel from the engine mounts, Sam trained a flashlight on the Rancor fuel filter.

"Damn."

Inside the clear oblong cylinder, the foot-tall filter was speckled with dirty dots of debris and water. If the fuel was contaminated after sitting so long, or water was mixed with it, it could do some serious damage to the injector pump, injector tip, and lines. Sam knew enough to guess what the problem was. He also knew enough to know he was going to have to get some help with replacing a fuel injector pump, an expensive proposition for both the labor and the parts.

"Great. Just what I needed."

Forgetting where he was, Sam stood up fast and banged his head on the inside ledge of a metal shelf inside the engine room. Cursing as he emerged, Sam closed the engine compartment door and replaced the companionway stairs. After cleaning himself up and changing his oil-soiled shirt, Sam locked the boat and climbed down into the dinghy. *Angel* didn't come with a scoop stern like some of its modern cousins, the Catalinas, and since Sam had previously lived aboard at dock, he'd never had a need for steps. Until now. Great. Another expense in the making.

Sam motored around the bend and into the marina. New finger piers jutted out from an equally new seawall, and high-end cruising boats were allotted the best spaces with smaller, older sailboats relegated to the lopsided wooden toothpick-like piers on the outer hinterlands of the 200-slip marina.

Tying up to a long pier near the waste pump-out station and fuel pumps, Sam found the dockmaster's office tucked inside a large white building that looked like it had been a house at one time, with its hip roofline and balcony outside a second-floor door.

Inside the building, Sam's eyes adjusted to the dark paneled interior lined with floor-to-ceiling bookshelves groaning from the weight of their contents. An ancient organ graced one wall, and on the opposite wall was a small television directed at the comfortable-looking wicker couches and chairs filling the space in between.

Sam smelled popcorn. He walked across the polished wooden floors toward the smell into a bright kitchen with hideous blue cabinets. A spindly man with a gray ponytail and matching beard greeted him without turning away from the microwave.

"Hello. Can I help you?"

"I'm looking for the dockmaster."

"Looks like you found him," the man said over his shoulder. "Name's Ed Caglioni. You need a slip?"

"If you could pull me into one, that'd be great. My engine died, so I anchored out in the creek. I'm guessing it's the fuel pump."

"Fuel pump, eh?" Ed pulled the finished popcorn out of the microwave and turned to face Sam. "What makes you think that?" He shoved a greasy hand into the bag of popcorn he was holding, then offered it to Sam.

Sam declined with a shake of his head, even though his stomach was growling loud enough to be heard.

"I checked everything else…. The filter's littered. I haven't been out in a while…."

"And you didn't know you were supposed to check it all out before you left the dock?" Ed interrupted crossly. "You know that's the most expensive part of the engine. What kind you got?"

Sam folded his arms. "I did check things before I left the dock, and everything was fine. And yes, I realize it's going to cost me. Can you help me or not?"

"Aww, don't get all upset. I just see so many people hop on boats without a clue about how to manage 'em. We don't need to pull you into a slip to fix it, though. That'll save you some money. Let's go look at the calendar and I'll see when I can get to it."

"Are you the only mechanic around?"

"I'm the only one you want working on your boat around here; I can tell you that." Ed strolled—no, strutted—across the sitting area of the clubhouse and into his office. "We got bathrooms with showers here, and washers and dryers, if you need 'em. Ordinarily, they're reserved for folks in the slips, but since I'm going to work on your boat, you can use 'em."

"Thanks. When do you think you can fit me in?"

Ed sounded suspiciously like Deputy Barney Fife from an old television show in his reply. "Weeeellll, I got a bottom job ahead of you, so it may be Tuesday before I can install it. What kind of an engine is it?"

"Volvo. I'll get the manual for you. Tuesday of next week?"

"Yep. That's the soonest I can get to it. I charge fifty bucks an hour, and once I get the part, it's gonna take me about a day. That suit you, er, what did you say your name is?" Ed motioned with the popcorn bag for Sam to sit in a ratty chair, unlike the fine ones out in the lounge area.

"Sam McClellan. And it has to be done." Sam sat down and stretched out his long legs.

"Where are you bound?"

"Norfolk."

"Edenton's a little out of the way," Ed offered as he filled out a work order form.

"I have an aunt here in town. I thought I'd come for a short visit."

"Oh? Who's your aunt?" Ed turned the paperwork around for Sam to sign and smiled a toothy grin under his popcorn-encrusted mustache like a shark about to take a bite of his prey.

"Lou McClellan. I haven't seen her since I was a kid, so I'll have to borrow your phonebook to find out where she lives."

Ed's smile suddenly vanished and his voice grew cold as he sat upright. "No need. She's on Oak Street, just a few blocks up from the river on the other side of our main street in town, which is actually Broad Street. You saw the dock at the foot of Broad when you sailed in, so it's a short walk from there." Ed paused for a second and leaned in toward

Sam conspiratorially so Sam could smell a mix of fuel and alcohol on his breath. "Are you coming now because of what she did?"

"What did she do?" Sam was puzzled.

"She murdered her neighbor. Nicest guy you wanta meet, and she turned her killer bees lose on him. Killed him just a few days ago. Says she didn't do it, but everyone in town knows she hated him."

"Why did she hate him?"

"Well, for years and years your dear aunt and Harvey Bishop were real friendly toward each other. They were so friendly, in fact, he'd asked her to marry him, town folk say. Well, she said she'd think about it. While she was thinking about it, his daughter shows up—a daughter he never knew he had—and Lou got all mad at him. She told everyone in town he was a pervert, and she was sick of being his neighbor. She was hoping to turn the town against him, but his family's been here a long, long time, and he wasn't about to go anywhere. He tried to calm her down, but she never did let up. So it don't surprise me one bit that she offed him."

"You seem to know a lot about the case," Sam said, standing up to leave.

"Yep, everybody knows all about it. Edenton is a small community. We're like a family, see. Sign here, and I'll order your pump."

"So you turn on one of your own just like that?" Sam glared at Ed Caglioni as he walked out without signing the work order.

"I can't order your part until you sign!" Ed called after him. "Look, I'm sorry about your aunt, but don't let that get in the way of getting your engine fixed."

Sam slammed the clubhouse door so hard the glass-paned door rattled as if it would shatter. Untying his dinghy's painter line from the dock, he hopped in and cranked the motor. Sam exited the marina, creating as much of a wake as his small two-stroke outboard could manage, and sped past his boat and down the creek toward the town docks.

Tying up to the *L*-dock he had passed on his way into the creek, Sam walked hurriedly along Water Street away from the main street Ed had told him about. He paid little attention to the well-kept stately homes that lined the waterfront.

Water Street curved away from the Albemarle Sound to become Oak Street, and Sam counted blocks until he covered two of them. When he saw the yellow police tape surrounding a white house with black shutters on the third block, he knew he was close.

As Sam approached the marked house, he took in its two neighbors. The one to the left was small, and a little too untidy for Sam to imagine it as his aunt's bed and breakfast. It had been years since he visited, so he wasn't quite sure of the address. The house on the right of the taped-off house was taupe with green-black shutters, green wicker furniture laden with wide Hunter green and white striped cushions on the wrap-around porch, and a green glider to match. Small wrought-iron occasional tables decorated with candles and flowers were on either side of every seat, making it apparent that this columned porch was designed for lounging. A small oval sign with barely legible letters was attached to the house. As Sam moved closer, he could make out the words: Lou's Inn. An overdrawn pink and white rose made the lettering hard to read, but perhaps that was the point.

A silver Toyota Camry was in the driveway, a narrow stretch of grass with parallel lines of concrete running its length. Sam saw the blue flicker of a television through lace curtains on the lower left window as he stepped up on the porch. Memories from childhood visits flooded his mind when he raised the brass fishtail knocker on the dark green front door.

CHAPTER THREE

Aunt Lou opened the door slowly, peering around it as if a goblin were on the other side.

"I already talked to the police," she huffed, and started to close the door.

"Aunt Lou?" Sam noticed the family resemblance immediately. Even in her bare feet, Lou stood nearly as tall as him, just like everyone else on his father's side of the family. Sam guessed her to be in her mid-seventies. "It's me, Sam McClellan. I've come to visit."

"Sammy? Oh, my, how grown up you are!" Lou pushed the door back wide and threw her arms around her nephew. "I have wondered for many years how you'd turn out, and it looks like you've turned out just fine. Come in, come in! You look thin. I'll fix us some lunch. I'm a little rusty, but can still whip something up...."

Sam followed his aunt through the sunny yellow foyer into a deep chocolate sitting room, and then into a well-used kitchen marked with blue and white as its color theme. Lou prattled on about how long it had been since she'd seen him, that she missed their visits, and urged him to fill her in on all that had happened since she last saw him as a child.

"Sit there at the counter," Lou said as she rounded the center kitchen island.

Sam did as he was told and sat on a tall white bar chair whose cushion had a print of blue and white fish swimming around its center. He offered to help, but Lou wouldn't hear of it.

"As long as I have breath, that's as far as anyone can come into *my* kitchen. When anyone comes snooping around my kitchen, going through my drawers, well, I just feel…violated. Everything has its place, after all, and nobody but me knows exactly how to put it all back," Lou defiantly explained. "I had it remodeled several years ago to my liking, and it suits me just fine. Now I don't want anyone messing about in here." Out of the refrigerator she pulled a plastic container of cold cuts, then mayonnaise, mustard, lettuce, pickles, bread, and a bowl of red grapes. She began to stack everything on the bread (minus the grapes), and decorated a glass plate with the sandwich, grapes, and pickles. She set Sam's place and a place beside him for herself at the counter. Lou fetched two glasses from a cupboard, filled them with ice, and poured tea from a small blue and white floral teapot into them. Lou fussed over a small flower arrangement that she placed in front of Sam and then set herself down on the adjacent bar chair.

"I had quite forgotten to eat lunch today," she said with her mouth full. "In fact, I believe I quite forgot to eat breakfast, too! See what happens when you get old, Sammy? The mind doesn't work so well anymore. But the spirit, it always stays young."

Sam devoured his food as Lou recited her aches and pains that seemed to have happened only last week. She didn't mention her neighbor or the news of his death, though she recounted many other tales of life in a small tourist town.

"Now see here," Lou said, leaning back in her chair and dabbing her napkin delicately at her mouth, "I've done all the talking. Tell me what you've been up to. I'll just clean up our plates while you talk." With that, she slipped to her feet like a cat off a perch and padded around the kitchen island to the sink.

"Well, I'm a little puzzled," Sam started. "When you opened the door, you said you'd already talked to the police. Were you expecting police to show up at your house?"

"Oh, that was silly. You looked so formal with your short hair and serious face, I just assumed you were another policeman."

"Another?"

Lou sighed and turned slowly away from the sink to face Sam. "Yes, another. Let's go sit in the living room." She wiped her wet hands on a blue and white fish towel, then took Sam by the hand and led him to the living room as if he needed help.

Sam could feel her bones through the paper-thin skin of her hand. Her hands were big like his, and her palm had noticeable calluses on it.

Lou let go of his hand and directed Sam to sit on the brown and white checked couch. The room looked like something out of a shelter magazine, some of which he'd flipped through while hanging out at his police partner's living room before his partner was murdered. Sam's late partner, Lee Evans, and his wife were always working on projects to fix up their place in Carolina Beach. They got a lot of their decorating ideas from magazines just like the ones Sam spotted on an ottoman in the corner. It seemed Lou did too.

"The whole town thinks I did it. I didn't do it, Sammy, and the more I tried to explain it, the worse it got."

"Did what, Aunt Lou?" Sam wanted Lou to tell him the story in her own words, rather than believe what Ed Caglioni had said.

"Harvey Bishop next door. He's dead. The police aren't sure about what happened, but there's talk that I did it."

"Tell me more."

"Harvey was attacked by a swarm of bees, and since I keep bees," Lou pointed a long boney finger toward a window opening to the backyard, "the town thinks I some-how managed to encourage my bees to attack, as if I could do that. I've told the police I keep domestic honey bees that are generally very docile unless aggravated, but these cops just don't know enough. They tried to take me in, but there aren't any accommodations for someone like me, so I'm being kept here under house arrest. They wanted to take the bees away, but they are all so scared to go near the hive, so they just left it here. It's all very silly, really. If they would just pay attention to what I've been saying, they'd realize I'm telling the truth. Can you imagine?"

"When did this happen?"

"Three days ago. Harvey had just been over here for lunch that day, and the next day, he was gone."

"Were you and Harvey friends?"

"We were the closest of friends for a long while. Then about three months ago, well, things changed." Lou looked down at her hands.

"How so?" Sam was attentive.

"Well, it's all very silly now, you know, but at the time, it seemed like the world had stopped. He, well, we were talking about getting married, and then just like you'd ask me to pass the salt and pepper, he informed me that he had a daughter. She's about your age, and since Harvey was never married, well, it was all such a shock. It took me a while to get used to the idea that Harvey had been, you know, wilder as a young man, but we were talking about getting married, and well, I just didn't know what to think. So between the time he told me about the young lady and a few days ago, we really weren't on speaking terms. That was about three months' time, which is a long time to go without speaking to your best friend. Well, just the other day, I invited him over for lunch to apologize for my attitude and to tell him I would accept his marriage proposal if he could find forgiveness in his heart for me. We had a delightful lunch and started planning our wedding that very afternoon. Then the next morning, well, he was gone! I don't know which is greater, the shock of his death, or the relief that I won't have to marry and move into his house!"

"So you didn't really love him all that much?"

"Oh, I don't know if it was love. For many, many years, we've been the best of friends, but when you get to be my age, you'll discover it's hard to change a zebra's stripes and all that. That's what we'd been talking about, and that was my hesitancy in getting married in the first place. And now they are going to take me off to the court to try me for his murder. Can you imagine? Me, a murderess?"

"No, I can't imagine it. And once we sift through the facts, we'll prove you didn't murder Harvey."

"You mean you'll help defend me? Are you a lawyer?"

"Not a lawyer. I just took a leave of absence from the Carolina Beach Police force."

"You're awfully young to retire, aren't you, Sammy?"

"I didn't really retire yet, but I'm thinking about it. Not everyone retires for the same reasons or at the same age,

Aunt Lou. I was just ready to do something else for a while. So I sailed here. I am on my way to Norfolk to see my son."

"You have a son?" Lou put her hand to her mouth. "You're so young, Sammy."

"I'm forty-two, Aunt Lou. I was married, and now my grown son is in the Coast Guard. Time flies, and all that. My engine conked out on me, and it's going to take time to fix it. I can't go anywhere until it's fixed, so I might as well help you get out of the jam you're in while I'm here." Sam took Lou's parchment-thin hand in his. "You've told me a little about what happened, and I'm sure if we dig a little deeper, we can find out what really happened to Harvey."

Lou's eyes welled up with tears. "Oh, Sammy—Sam, if you could help me, I would greatly appreciate it." Lou looked at Sam with sincere appreciation.

Sam couldn't believe she was capable of murder. He pulled his wallet out of his back pocket and rooted for a card. "Here's my cell number. You can call me day or night, Aunt Lou, and I'll be here in nothing flat. I anchored my boat in the creek on the way into the marina, so I'll get back and forth in my dinghy."

"Sam, you are so sweet to help me. But whatever can I do in return? You need anything while you're in town, you just speak up."

"Well, I do need some groceries. May I borrow your car?"

"Certainly. I can't drive it anyway, now that I'm under house arrest. It's actually kind of thrilling. I've never been in the spotlight before. All these years running my house as a bed and breakfast inn, I wanted publicity. I'd get an occasional story in the local newspaper, and my place even got written up in a fancy magazine once—but that was years ago. I haven't had a guest here in about four years. I've had 'specials' on rooms, and I even got one of the local boat owners to arrange for sunset cruises, but the business has fallen off, and it surely won't be back after this mess."

"You never know, Aunt Lou," Sam smiled. "Sometimes, a little notoriety is just the thing to give a boost to business."

"We'll see," she said. "I may be about done with business at this point. And as much as I'd like to leave this town, I'm not sure I'd want to move at my age. I've heard of people going on extended cruises on those big ocean liners. I've read in a magazine where it's actually cheaper to do that than it is to go into a nursing home—plus, I bet it's a whole lot more fun." Lou giggled like a school girl. "Maybe that's what I'll do as soon as you figure out what happened to Harvey. Thank you for your help, Sam. It means a lot to me." Lou hugged Sam gently.

Sam carefully embraced Lou, afraid to squeeze her too tightly. He helped her up from her seat, then walked with her to the front door.

Lou gave Sam her car key and a key to the house, insisting that he stay with her while he was in town.

Unable to (and not wanting to) turn her down, Sam promised to return with some clothes. He took with him

Lou's grocery list, and walked back to the waterfront dock where his dinghy was waiting.

Sam motored back to his boat, startling Kathy as he climbed aboard. "Might want to go find some other place, Kathy. I'm not going to be here for a few days, so no company for you."

Kathy didn't budge.

Sam stuffed a duffel bag full of clothes and grabbed his cellphone. After securing *Angel*, he climbed over the aft rail and gently lowered himself into the dinghy.

Sam motored back to the town dock, then thought better of it and motored farther up Queen Anne's Creek. He could see Oak Street from the water and continued past it as well. Motoring under a short bridge, then under the remains of an old rusty railroad bridge, Sam entered a cypress-lined passage that dumped into a narrow cove. A relatively new dock jutted out through a forest of cypress knees and Spanish moss. Sam tied up to the dock. Walking on a long, narrow boardwalk over the black-water swamp, Sam noted a few water snakes slithering about under the lily pads and other water plants.

An old mill building-turned-swank condos was advertised on a huge billboard attached to the brick building, with renderings of what one of the luxury condos looked like ("original hardwood floors, windows, and skylights add to the luxury of these upscale condos" read the caption).

"Own a piece of history," Sam snorted when he read the price range. Sam hoofed it along a road dotted with renovated mill houses bordering the creek. Only one holdout still had its original porch and wood frame, albeit listing to one side. Sam marveled at the amount of money it probably took to bring one of these old mill houses up to code.

Back at Lou's, Sam cranked up the Camry. With Lou's grocery list in his pocket and directions on where to shop, the thought of a home-cooked meal made Sam's mouth water as he drove.

CHAPTER FOUR

Aunt Lou showed off her cooking skills that evening, serving chicken with sun-dried tomatoes over penne pasta with port wine cream sauce and a side of crisp asparagus tips lightly sautéed in butter. Even though Sam complained of a full stomach after his third helping as he pushed away from the linen-clad dining table, Lou wouldn't hear of it.

"Dinner isn't over until the dessert plates are cleared, and it's been so long since I've had company to cook for, you'll just have to suffer through it," Lou said as she brought out a double-layer carrot cake with cream cheese frosting decorated with squiggly ribbons of orange icing.

"My lines are not as straight as they used to be," Lou complained. "In fact, my writing looks like a four-year-old's first attempt at letters! I remember how proudly you showed yours off to me one time when you and your parents came to visit. How are your folks?"

"They're fine. They live in Raleigh. I don't see them as often as I probably should. But then again, the road goes both ways."

"That's all very well and good, Sam, but you are on a boat now, and I gather there's not much of a guest room aboard that would encourage them to come and visit, now is there?"

Sam looked down at his plate. "No, I guess not. I'll make plans to visit them as soon as I get back from Norfolk."

"Tell me about your son. You said he's there?"

"He's in the Coast Guard. He was in California for his last tour of duty, and then he got transferred to Norfolk. I don't really know what he's doing. We didn't keep up with each other for a while there."

"Making up for lost time? Well, the sooner the better, I say. You never know exactly what fates lie in wait."

"Aunt Lou," said Sam gently, "it may not be any of my business, but exactly what happened between you and Dad? I remember coming here when I was small, but then we stopped coming, and Dad wasn't interested in telling me what happened. Will you?"

Lou hesitated. "It's a long story. Ancient history. Not worth getting into tonight."

"Well, if it's ancient history, perhaps you could call Dad and patch things up?" Sam worked hard to get the last bite of carrot cake into his mouth.

"Perhaps." Lou wasn't volunteering.

Sam wasn't going to push further, so he thanked her for the dinner and started to clear the table.

"My kitchen, my rules. I have a system, remember?"

"Yes, ma'am." Sam felt like he was in high school again. He ran his fingers through his short dark hair as he watched Lou slowly clear the table. She stood straight up, but her gait was slow. If she had done any harm to her neighbor, it would have taken a long time to get it done.

"Is there a mechanic in town who might be able to help me with my engine?" Sam took a seat at the kitchen island and watched his aunt slowly scrape and clean the plates.

"Al's Auto Body is a few blocks away. You might not want to mention you are staying with me, if you want to get anything done."

"So I've noticed. There's not a boat supply place in town that you know of, is there?"

"There was one at the marina, but they closed down. The owners sold out to a condo developer, and they wanted to have a cutesy sea-wares shop in that building, but they can't seem to get any takers. This town's changed quite a bit with all the condos coming in, but you can't blame them. The water, the historic town, it's just a perfect combination for developers. Even Harvey was thinking of selling out."

"What did Harvey do?"

"Oh, it's not what he did so much, but what he had. His family owned the last functioning menhaden plant up on the Chowan River. Harvey was still running it as a fish cannery, and a very successful one, too. He told me several of the condo developers had approached him, wanting to buy the property because of where it sat. I'd been up there a number of times to get my fish. It's so much better than getting it at the grocery store where it's grown in farms in places I've never heard of, and they had all types of fresh local seafood and crab. You can run up there tomorrow, if you like. I'd love to go with you, but I'm under house arrest, remember?"

"Yes, I remember. I would like to see it. Is it still open?"

"Not yet. Harvey was going up there every day to work. He never missed a day of work in his life. His staff closed for the week out of respect. And to figure out what they're going to do now that he's gone."

"Did Harvey own the property outright?"

"Yes. So his lawyer's gotten himself into the middle of it, sifting through three offers from developers who showed up the second the news of Harvey's death hit the street. Honestly, you'd think they'd show a little more respect."

"You'd think. Are the developers all from Edenton?"

"One is; the others aren't. How they caught wind of it, I'll never know."

"And how did his long-lost daughter take all of this?"

"I haven't the foggiest. You should ask her yourself."

"She's here? In Edenton?"

"Yes. She's a real estate agent with one of the agencies in town. Like I said earlier, Harvey told me about her only a few months ago, but she's been in town for a while now. Why she didn't come forward sooner, I don't know. Her name is Monica Maples. I don't know which agency she's with, but you could pick up one of the color books and find her."

"Color book?"

"You know, those little booklets filled with color pictures of all the homes for sale. You can find plenty of them on Broad Street. Most all the agents have their pictures and names by their property listings. It's a hot market. I am simply amazed by what people are listing their houses for… now that's not to say they are getting their asking prices, but who knows? The condos are outrageously priced in my opinion, and they are selling out fast."

"You know a lot about the real estate business, Auntie."

"Well, when you get to be my age, you'll find it's wise to keep up with who's selling and at what price. You never know when that kind of information will come in handy. Besides, I may want to sell this place someday. I suspect I'll have enough to cruise around the world for the rest of my days, and leave something to God knows who."

"Special charities, perhaps?"

"Oh, I don't know. I dream up lots of ways to spend my money, but I haven't spent any yet. I had a successful business for decades here, and aside from a few upgrades, I haven't spent much. So when I sell the house, I could easily afford to do whatever I wanted."

"Sounds like you can afford to do that now."

"What I want is to clear my name of this mess. Then I'll make some decisions."

"A good plan," Sam nodded. A quick look at the window confirmed his thoughts. "It's still light out. You mind if I take a walk?"

"No, I don't mind at all. I wish I could join you, but walks are tiring to me these days. And then, there's the house arrest…."

"I agree. I'll be back in a bit."

"That's fine. Let yourself in with the key I left for you on the front hall table, and lock up behind you." With that, Lou waved Sam off and retired to her bedroom.

Heading back toward the waterfront, Sam strolled the two short blocks from Oak to Broad Street. The moist evening air felt heavy to Sam as he took in a sky of orange and purple with streaks of golden sun filtering through the clouds. The Sound was mirror-flat calm, and only the hum of a distant motorboat broke the music of birds settling in for the night in the crape myrtles along Water Street.

The town dock had three large powerboat cruisers plugged into electrical outlets on finger piers, and a long sailboat cozied up to the inside of the concrete breakwater.

Evening walkers were doing a loop around a green water-front park and onto the pier to gawk at the boats. A rift of Bob Marley competed for attention with children's squeals of laughter tumbling from the direction of a swing set in the park. Sam took it all in like a dry sponge absorbing water for the first time. So this was one of the pleasures of cruising he'd never experienced before. All things familiar set in a strange place, Sam fell into the cadence of the evening and strolled the park loop, too.

At the far end of the park was a small lighthouse structure. Upon closer inspection, Sam was able to read a sign indicating this screw-pile lighthouse was one of the last of its kind in the state. Information about its renovation and interpretive tour times was posted, though the lighthouse looked buttoned up for the night.

Heading up Broad Street, Sam walked by the first of many real estate businesses pinched into offices in brightly painted buildings dating back to an earlier century. A few spirited people in animated conversation spilled out of a two-story restaurant with what looked like the hulk of a tugboat on its rooftop visible from the street. Aside from the few restaurants dotting this main street through the historic town, businesses were closed for the night. Sam noted a coffee shop on the other side of the street; he thought that might be a good place to try in the morning.

Picking up two color books showing property listings from a small upright rack in front of one of the real estate offices, Sam continued on his way west down a promising side street. He was not disappointed. Mansions—no, former plantation manors—lined the street in perfect unison. Fat-trunked trees on one side, though, missed their companions, and the lopsided canopy told of a hurricane that must have taken prisoners. Sam remembered Hurricane Isabel visiting the coast a few years earlier, but since there was little impact on Carolina Beach, he didn't think much of it. *Funny how it's only the immediate storms we worry about*, he thought. This one had left a calling card for Edenton. Though the town's buildings seemed undamaged, the trees told a different story.

Doubling back toward town, Sam met other walkers and an occasional bicycler on the grid streets of Edenton. When he got to Queen Street, he noted three bed and breakfasts right in a row. Competition for Auntie, no doubt. One advertised on a sign that sunset cruises were available. If they were that popular, perhaps he should hire out his boat. Or not. People on his boat might not like the idea of a first mate duck. Sam knew he didn't.

Nearing Aunt Lou's street, Sam took a side trip to the creek to check on his dinghy. Not knowing the tide here, Sam doubled the lines and locked the motor in place. Night was fast approaching, and in the dark cypress swamp, not much light shown through the trees. Slowly walking along the narrow boardwalk, Sam felt the edge of the wooden slats with his foot before taking another step. Finally out of the swamp, Sam followed the aura of the accent lights pointed toward the Mill condos until he was on the street again.

Walking through the Mill Village, Sam heard the sounds of nighttime from the open screened windows and porches of the 1,000 square-foot mill houses—what Sam noted in a color book were referred to as cottages. From some of the cottages, Sam could hear parents calling for kids to get in the bath or go to bed, but most small cottages had folks sitting on porches visiting in the cooling night with their neighbors. Sam guessed them to be retired or soon to be, with their pipes aglow and snow-on-the-roof heads. A few hands went up in casual waves to Sam, and he returned the greeting. Life in a genteel Southern town, where everyone waves and says hello, was so much different from the tourist-filled town of Carolina Beach he'd called home for years.

Mosquitoes were out for blood, so Sam quickened his step toward Oak Street, just a short walk away. It was dark now, and Sam noticed lights in all the houses dotting Oak Street. All houses, except one.

Harvey's house was dark. Sam's debate with himself was a short one. Yes, he'd be breaking and entering. Yes, he might be seen. But…he might also find evidence that the local police force overlooked—evidence that could be helpful in clearing Lou's name. A long shot, but not out of the question. Walking around the house to the backyard, Sam talked himself into finding a way in so he could see the crime scene for himself. Wadding up his hand in the bottom of his untucked shirt, he tried a door. Locked. Through a screened porch, Sam saw another door. Gently leaning into the lower screen of one side of the porch, Sam was able to gain entry. Again using his shirt to keep his fingerprints to himself, Sam tried the door. It was locked, but the frame was not secure in its jam. With a little more prying, Sam was into the house with the door quietly closing behind him.

Sam felt his way through the narrow hall. Tapping gently at a large hollow metal box and then another beside it, Sam guessed he was in the laundry room. Coming into another room, Sam was relieved to have a little moonlight, and the glow of a street light filtered through the room's curtains to help him find his way in the dark. A long couch consumed one entire wall of the cramped room, a musty smell filling Sam's nostrils. Opposite the couch was a boxy old-fashioned television set with rabbit ears on it. Sam noted it seemed out of place, given how most of the world was digital—everything these days. A bookcase crammed with musty-smelling books bordered a door on either side; tumbles of books were everywhere on the floor.

Sam walked into the adjoining room, a kitchen with an old wide porcelain sink with grooves in its side used for draining plates. Tiled countertops were empty of canisters, appliances, or other tips to daily cooking. There was, however, a large and relatively new coffee maker, and from the smell of it, one that hadn't been cleaned in several days. No dirty dishes in the sink, no scrunched up towels on a counter, and no boxes of cereal in the cabinets. Either Harvey wasn't much of a cook, or he needed some serious groceries.

Sam found his way back into the cramped living room and into a small foyer. Judging from the outside, Harvey's house was about the same size as Aunt Lou's, but the configuration was probably closer to its original 1920s construction: chopped up, small rooms, no closets. Lou's house, on the other hand, had seen major renovations at some point to make it feel spacious and open. Sam understood now why Lou had hesitated to marry Harvey, if moving into his house was part of the package.

Sam found the staircase. But before he started up, his elbow brushed against a thin strip of police tape strung across a closed adjacent door. The crime scene. Of course. That would make sense. Harvey's room was downstairs, like Lou's. At their age, there would be no desire to climb stairs.

Sam felt his way around the room. A streetlight on Oak Street offered sufficient illumination of this bedroom on the front of the house, and it was as cluttered as the rest of Harvey's home. Books tripped and tumbled over each other on two side tables. More were scattered about the floor like a tornado-twisted library. An old fishing creel hung from a peg, and a fishing pole leaned against it. Dark checkered curtains puddled on the floor, and a stack of books towered under the window. Using his elbow, Sam grazed the top of the window lock. The metal catch was unlocked.

Moving out of the room and then out of the house the same way he came in, Sam crept along the outside of the house to stand under Harvey's window. To get in, Sam could hoist himself up. He'd have an easier time if he stood on something, though. And surely his aunt wouldn't be able to make it through the window, though she might have a key to the house.

With the back of his hand, Sam felt the window screen. There were no slices or breaks that he could feel. As he moved his hand around the screen's edges, he felt the distinct prick of protruding metal sharp enough to catch his attention along with his finger. A few passes back and forth over the same spot and Sam knew what he was feeling. The screen had been stapled in several places back into its wooden casing. Before he could inspect it further, Sam heard a car door shut nearby and ducked, hoping he wasn't seen. He'd have to get a closer look in daylight to determine when this repair job had been made.

After a few minutes, Sam found his way to the tall privacy fence separating Harvey's yard from Lou's. Toward the back of the narrow lot was a break in the fence, a deliberate space where the points of neighboring lots beside and behind Harvey's house came together. Each fence dipped to waist high from its adjoining eight-foot sections. Sam had never seen such a glacier-like drop in fences before. Hopping the fence into Lou's backyard, Sam immediately heard the dull sound of buzzing emanating from three stacked hives. Sam backed away, his back rubbing up against the fence that bordered the back of Lou's yard. Sam moved along it until he reached the other end, where he again found a dip in the fence's corner just like at the other side, this one opening the dark view to the side and back neighbors' yards. Odd.

A few lights were on at each of the houses surrounding Lou's. Not wanting to disturb anyone, Sam followed the fence to the front of Lou's house, climbed the porch steps, and let himself in for the night. He'd have to make the same tour another time in the daylight.

CHAPTER FIVE

Sam woke to the sounds of pans clanging in the kitchen. The smell of cooking bacon drifted up the stairs, finding Sam outstretched on a queen-sized Victorian bed. Its high headboard pointed toward the ten-foot ceilings of a pale blue room, and from Sam's vantage point of the headboard, the elaborate carving of birds and ribbons soared in flight.

Sam took in his surroundings: he saw linens on a bedside table of dark mahogany that matched the bed, a quilt rack draped with two quilts similar in color scheme of yellow and blue but different in patterns, a dresser cluttered with porcelain figurines blocking a view to its attached mirror, and a fluffy chair skirted in a red and blue floral print. Two tall windows graced the room with sunlight, reminding Sam he was a guest, even if he was family.

Hastily pulling on his jeans and a fresh T-shirt from his duffle bag, Sam headed downstairs. The ornately carved handrail's paint was chipping, giving clues to the many colors it had been blessed with over decades.

Lou ignored Sam's entrance into the kitchen, carrying on with breakfast preparations. Dressed and coiffed, Lou decorated plates with grapes, watermelon slices, and twists of oranges. The garnishes surrounded a heap of pancakes topped with whipped cream and a cherry. Perfectly cooked bacon crisscrossed a serving plate, slightly hiding the blue and white fish motif.

Lou placed the loaded plate in front of Sam at the kitchen's island bar and waited expectedly for him to comment.

Sam didn't disappoint. "Wow! What a fantastic-looking meal! You must have been up for hours. You didn't have to go to all that trouble."

"Oh, it's no trouble. I love to cook, and to have company to cook for is just the best thing for me. Did you sleep well?"

"Yes. It's been a while since I slept in a bed. I've been living aboard for a number of years, and even though I have a spring mattress on my bunk, there's still such a difference. I slept like a log."

"Good. That's what I like to hear. Now eat up. There's plenty more if you need seconds."

"Aren't you going to join me?" Sam noted a second place setting at the ready beside his.

"No, I already had my banana and coffee. Do you like your coffee with cream and sugar?"

"Just black, thanks." Sam felt guilty only for a second about eating in front of her, but the first bite of banana pancakes smothered in rich maple syrup propelled him through his guilt and through the rest of the stack.

Lou poured coffee into an oversized mug decorated with a blue-and-white fish; then she bustled in the kitchen, cleaning up the bacon pan. The rest she'd cleaned and put away before Sam had entered the room.

"I don't usually serve breakfast in the kitchen, but since there's only one of you, and you are family after all, I thought this would be all right."

"It's definitely all right with me. Remember, I live on a boat. When I eat, I eat in my living room, my kitchen, and my workshop. It's all the same room. Your home is palatial by comparison."

"I've enjoyed it. The two bedrooms upstairs have held all kinds of guests. Artists, sailors, writers, politicians… they've all stayed here. Once, Dan Rather stayed here. He was much younger then, and he was covering a story. You may have heard about it. One of the daycare centers in town was shut down after the owners were accused of molesting the children."

"I remember reading about it. Did it have a bad impact on the town?"

"For a short time, perhaps. But it did create quite a stir. Edenton was a household name then, and we were in the spotlight. It took several years to live down the reputation of being a harbor for pedophiles, but just as the media tore us down for that, they helped rebuild our reputation by claiming that Edenton is the prettiest small town in the South. The recent recession hit us as hard as it did other places, especially since most of our people here are retirees or work for the service-driven businesses that support them, but I've noticed that things are starting to bounce back, and once again, real estate prices are climbing. The biggest indicator of this town's health is the number of visitors we get in the spring who soon choose to become residents."

"Sounds like another beach town I know. Carolina Beach has had its share of good and bad times. It seems to be in a perpetually upward spiral right now, even though pundits say the real estate market can't keep going up."

"I hear that too, but I see no signs of a slowdown here in Edenton. Do you like our little park and the dock at the waterfront?" Sam nodded as he took another bite of bacon. "It's relatively new. There's a nice bathhouse for boaters to use, and that Roanoke River lighthouse has been a huge attraction for people who tour the coast to appreciate all of North Carolina's lighthouses. That particular screw-pile lighthouse was someone's home for years, and its past is almost as colorful as the fellow who used to own it. You might want to visit it while you're here, Sammy. It started out in Plymouth back in the 1800s because that was such a vital shipping town. It's hard to imagine now, considering it's such a little town, but once upon a time, Plymouth was really important to the development of our state because of its location on the Roanoke River. That river runs over four hundred miles inland, all the way up to the Blue Ridge Mountains, and dumps into the Albemarle Sound, so it was an incredibly important river for shipping goods. Ships provided the fastest way to move cargo. But railroads and highways changed all that. When it was no longer needed, the lighthouse was decommissioned and sold for ten dollars to a private citizen in the 1950s. He bought two other lighthouses for the same price, then proceeded to lose them in the Sound when he was attempting to move them. A tugboat operator purchased this last one before it saw the same fate. After he passed away, the lighthouse was purchased and floated in to its current location and restored." Lou chuckled. "It's rather ironic. Where it sits is not too far from where an old tugboat came into town about twenty years ago for restoration. It sank before serious work could be done. It's like the tug hit the shore without that lighthouse in place!"

"I didn't see a tugboat when I took my walk last night."

"That's because it was towed out to sea and sunk to create an artificial reef," Lou said. "Edenton's history is so much more than colonial."

The doorbell rang. Lou ambled to the door, her gait a little slower than yesterday's. Sam followed, coffee cup in hand.

"Morning, James. Coffee's hot. Help yourself." Lou opened the door wide, allowing an overweight, balding policeman in full uniform to come in. "James Bradley, this is my nephew, Sam McClellan. He's here for a short visit while he gets his boat engine repaired."

Sam stepped forward and shook James' hand.

"Welcome to Edenton. First time here?" James walked with Sam, just two steps behind Lou, who headed back to the kitchen and pointed to the bar chairs.

"It's been a while since I visited Aunt Lou. The town doesn't look like it's changed much between visits."

"In appearance, no, I guess it doesn't change much. We get a lot of turnover in people, though. There's a bunch of long-time families who will never leave, like mine. But lots of people come to town, think, 'Oh, it's so pretty here,' stay for a while, then move on."

"Carolina Beach has the same. I see a lot of turnover there, too," said Sam, joining in the small talk while waiting to hear the reason James was present.

Lou served James a cup of coffee, milky white with real cream. As she set it down, James' face lit up. For a moment, he sipped the hot brew.

"Ah, thanks, Lou. It's just the way I like it."

"Come here often?" Sam sat down beside James.

"Oh, every morning for years," Lou answered for James. "I had a break-in back in…when was it, James, 1982? Since then, James has been coming like clockwork to check on me and have coffee before he starts his shift. I must say, though, that we seem to have much more to talk about since Harvey's death," piped Lou. "You're visits are now part of my house arrest; isn't that right, James?"

"Yeah, just making sure you've not flown the coop." James winked at Lou. Then he turned to Sam. "Besides, she makes the best coffee in Edenton. So you've had engine trouble? What happened?"

"I think it's the fuel pump. Today I'm going to see if I can find a mechanic to help me."

"Ol' Ed couldn't fix it?"

"Ed Caglioni at the marina seemed really busy," Sam lied. "Besides, this gives me an excuse to catch up with my aunt."

"Well, you couldn't have picked a better time, seeing as how she's got to stay put for a while."

"James, how long exactly *do* I have to stay put?" Lou looked chastened.

"As long as it takes to clear this mess up."

"Well, I hope it won't take long; I need to keep a hair appointment." Lou crossed her arms.

"We're working on it, Lou," James offered. "Do you still have some of that blueberry pie?"

"No. I have something better. I fixed this for Sam when he arrived last night. It's fresh." Lou pulled the double-layer carrot cake with cream cheese icing out of the refrigerator. "Do you want some, Sammy?"

"No thanks, Lou. I'm stuffed." Sam turned to watch James dive into his piece of cake with a vengeance. "So what have you found out?"

Between bites, James answered, dabbing his mouth with a napkin Lou provided. "Well, we are sure he died from a bee sting, or something akin to it. That's according to the coroner. At first, we thought it was just a heart attack, but then we found a bunch of dead bees beside his bed, so it seemed necessary to see if there was anything else going on."

"What makes you think it was Lou's bees that did this?"

"Well, it's mostly a matter of proximity," James said, icing dripping out of the corner of his mouth. "She keeps the bees right next to his side of the fence."

"Well, wouldn't that be an accident if bees were getting into his house?" Sam was taking mental notes.

"Some folks, like me, do think it was just an accident. But the town is looking for a quick resolve to keep Edenton out of the national spotlight. The bad press might ruin the real estate market. Anyway, it's just hard to match what killed him to the bees that Lou keeps because nobody but her can get near them to take a sample. The chief thinks that to ask her to do it is asking her to tamper with the evidence."

"So a case has been built against Lou based on the proximity of her beehives to her neighbor's house. That's not much of a case, if you ask me," Sam gulped his coffee. "I mean, how do you know there's anything more than just a random bee that snuck into his house?"

"Well, talk around town would suggest that she didn't like Harvey one bit. And the old saying of a woman scorned…."

"I wasn't *scorned*, James." Lou braced her fists on the table as she spoke. "I told you what happened. I was the one who scorned Harvey. Besides, we were getting along much better and were talking about getting married. Why in heaven's name would I want to kill the man I had just agreed to marry?"

"For the money?" James winked again and wiped his chin. "Harvey owned a good deal of land out on River Way, after all, Lou. That's your motive."

Lou played along. "You are assuming he put me in his will, and then he told me about it. Otherwise, I wouldn't have any idea that I might benefit from his death. If that were the case, I would indeed have a motive. Let's just think this through, shall we? I snuck into his house in the middle of the night and let out a jar of bees, but not before whispering in all their little ears to go sting Harvey. Then I slipped out without getting stung myself, and came home to make myself a cup of tea. Is that how I did it?"

"Something like that. You have a key to his house, so slipping in after dark wouldn't have been a problem. You're used to bee stings, so even if you did get stung, it wouldn't have been any big deal to you. And you happen to like tea, so why not have a cup when you get home from doing your dirty work?" James was all smiles as he laid out the murder of Harvey Bishop.

Sam wasn't sure whether James were friend or foe. "Only three holes in your theory, Officer. First, according to Lou, she's not hurting for money. Second, you are implying she had knowledge of Harvey's will, and that she knew she was going to inherit everything. Did you, Aunt Lou?"

"Harvey said he had a will, but it wasn't something we discussed. No, I had no knowledge of the contents of his will."

"Okay, so that won't fly, James. And third, Lou goes to bed before the sun sets. I was here last night and saw her enter her room right after dinner. She'd not be able to do it the way you said because she'd be asleep by the time Harvey died. What time did you say he died?"

"I didn't, but we put the time of death a little after two in the morning. Look, Sam; I really am on Lou's side. I think the whole thing is preposterous, so don't get upset with me. Lou and I have played this little game every morning since it happened."

Lou nodded to confirm she knew it was just a game.

"I'm here as much for her company as for my job; that's all. Nothing to get upset about. We'll find out what happened; then we can all go back to the way things were."

"Things will never be the same for Lou, James," Sam interjected. "Her reputation is shot after this."

"Oh, that's not necessarily so, Sammy. I expect I enjoy the notoriety. Might even get some business out of it." Lou laughed. "Don't go getting your boxers in a wad. We're just having fun." Lou poured James another cup of coffee and topped off Sam's.

Turning to James, Lou said, "Sam just retired from the Carolina Beach Police force, James. Perhaps he could help you find out what happened?"

"Sure, Lou. We're always happy to have a fellow cop around the station. Retired, huh? And cruising on a yacht? You guys must get paid a whole lot more than us." James smiled sincerely.

"No. I always lived on the boat, and I was ready to do something different. I didn't really retire, yet, just took a leave of absence. I thought sailing for a few weeks might help me decide what comes next. Only problem is I can't go far with my motor all messed up."

"What do you need a motor for if it's a sailboat?"

"To get in and out of anchorages, mostly, and if there's a day without wind."

James snorted. "You won't find many of those around here. Listen; why don't you come around to the station with me now?" James looked at his watch. "I have to get on in, and I could give you a ride."

Lou chimed in. "Yes, do go, Sam. You might be able to help James. I'll be fine without you here. You just come back and get the car whenever you want to go see the mechanic."

"Which mechanic?" James asked over a slurp of coffee. "Al's Auto Shop?"

"Yes. I think if we don't spread it around that he's staying here with me, he'll get by just fine. Now you two run along. I want to clean the house."

"The house is already clean, Lou." James headed for the door. "Don't overdo."

"I'll be down in a minute," Sam called as he headed upstairs to get ready for the day. James seemed all right. No need to worry about Lou with him around.

CHAPTER SIX

Sam joined James in the car for the short ride to the police station located on a prime waterfront lot down by the town's marina. James shared a little of Edenton's history, pointing to houses with wrap-around porches and well-manicured lawns as he drove. The early morning sun shimmered on the bay, and a few people were out for morning strolls with their dogs in the park. Standing directly in front of the station in the median was a revolutionary war hero's statue. Across the street and sitting smack on the water was a colonial house-turned-museum, the Barker House. Ample parking graced both sides of the street, but James pulled into the best lot of all, one nestled behind the station fronting the park and town docks.

"Is your boat in here?" James nodded to the slips of the waterfront dock as they got out of the car.

"No, I'm anchored out in the creek that goes into the marina. These docks are more convenient, but I need to anchor out as much as possible. That's how I'm able to cruise."

"That makes sense. Where are you going?"

"Norfolk, for starters. My son's stationed there."

"Navy?"

"Coast Guard. He just transferred from California, so I haven't seen him in a few years."

"Where will you go after that?" James asked as he parked the car.

"Don't know, exactly. I'm thinking it would be fun to sail the Chesapeake Bay. I haven't been to a boat show, and there's one in October. Maybe I'll hit that." Sam followed James up the steps to the porch of the brick station. It looked proper enough to be a colonial house, with dark-green shutters and a few rocking chairs on a columned porch angled toward the water.

The interior was as crisp as the outside, with a main reception desk jutting out into the lobby.

"Morning, Annabelle," James called to the small woman behind the high-countered reception desk. "Need a name badge for my friend here."

"Dragging 'em in off the street, now, James?" the receptionist Annabelle Withers asked, smiling. "What's your name, honey?"

"Sam McClellan."

Annabelle put down her pen and glared at Sam. "Any relation to Lou McClellan?"

"She's my great-aunt. I'm visiting her for a few days." Sam leaned on the elbow-high counter of the receptionist's desk.

"Annabelle, mind your manners," James cheerfully chimed. "Sam is an officer from Carolina Beach. He might be able to help us find out exactly what happened to Mr. Bishop."

"You are admitting that we need help?" Annabelle's graying eyebrows were plucked in permanent surprise. "James, shame on you." Annabelle handed Sam his name badge and smiled a toothy smile. "Harvey was *my* cousin. Distant cousin, but a cousin, nonetheless. You'll find that many of us are related by birth or by marriage here, except for the tourists who come and stay for a while. I would like nothing better than to find out who did this to my cousin."

"Sorry for your loss," Sam soothed. "Did Harvey have lots of cousins?"

"There are about ten that I know of, but I'm the last remaining one," Annabelle shook her gray head. "All gone, every one."

"Plus one daughter that we know of," Sam added.

"That's right. That was a shocker. Didn't know old Harvey had it in him, but he was as shocked as the rest of us. Poor Harvey, God rest his soul."

"My condolences, Annabelle." Sam patted her pudgy hand and followed James through a set of double doors. Inside was a large glossy-white, window-rimmed room filled with metal desks and green cushioned chairs standing in line like kindergartners waiting to go to recess. At the far end of the room were two young uniformed policemen putting on bicycle helmets.

James raised his hand in salute to them. "Morning, fellas." Then turning to Sam, he said, snorting, "That's the way we catch the bad guys these days. They ride bicycles all day long. A younger man's game, it is." James patted his expanded girth.

"Carolina Beach has bike patrols, too," said Sam, answering the unasked question. "It helps to stay visible. That patrol came along after I made detective, so I didn't participate either." Sam followed James to a far corner office—a waterfront one. James knocked twice on the glossy white six-panel door, then pushed the door open without waiting to be asked in. "Morning, Chief. Got someone I think you ought to meet." James stepped aside and nodded to Sam to enter.

"Sam McClellan." Sam strode to the desk in front of him to shake hands with Edenton's Chief of Police. His cigarette-stained teeth and paunch made Sam guess him to be about fifteen years older than himself.

"Matt Harris. You new to town?" Matt sat down again in his groaning wood-slated chair. It wasn't like the ones out front.

"You could say that. I'm visiting my aunt. James offered to introduce me around the station when we met this morning."

"He's Lou's nephew, Chief," added James. "He took a leave of absence from the Carolina Beach Police force, and I thought he might be some help to us since he's staying with her."

"Lou's nephew, eh?" Matt leaned back in his chair. "Well, a fine welcome you're getting. Sorry for the house arrest thing. Have a seat," Matt said, motioning to a sagging couch opposite his desk. "Thank you, James." Matt waved James off without looking at him as if he were shooing away a bothersome picnic-intruding fly.

Sam sat on a short faux-leather couch opposite Matt's ornately-carved desk with modesty panel to match. He quickly glanced around the office, noting faded black-and-white framed photographs of a younger man shooting baskets, whom he assumed was Matt. There was uniformed Matt shaking hands with the governor, and one with him on a boat surrounded by fishing buddies helping him hold the biggest tuna Sam had ever seen.

"You've obviously heard Lou's side of the story at this point." Matt waited, fingers confidently folded on his desk.

"She said she didn't understand what all the fuss was about. Can you tell me about your investigation?"

"Well, so far, there's not much to tell. Lou was the one who reported Mr. Bishop's death. She said she called him to ask him to come unstop a sink one morning, and he didn't answer. She looked out the window, saw his car, and decided he'd slept in too long that day. She marched over there, used a key she has had for years, and let herself in, only to discover Harvey still in bed. But when she shook him, he didn't wake up, and his face looked 'different' to her than usual. She high-tailed it out of there and called 9-1-1. Of course, it was too late when they arrived."

"So an old man died in his sleep. What's so unusual about that?" Sam leaned forward, matching the Chief's posture as closely as he could.

"The autopsy showed venom in his bloodstream. There were carcasses of bees around Harvey and two on the floor. There were no tears in his window screens, no signs of forced entry. If he'd been stung during the previous day and had a bad reaction to it, he would have gotten himself to the hospital. Harvey was a regular at Doc Ward's office."

"And since Aunt Lou had a key to his house, and loads of bees, you're just sure she did it." Sam sank back into the couch.

"We're not saying that exactly. She had talked him down around town for months before this happened, so they weren't on the best of terms. She did have easy access to him, and she certainly has enough of the critters to cause a stir. According to a local expert, all anybody would have to do to get bees in a tizzy is to put them in a paper sack and shake the sack up before releasing them. Then they'd sting just about anything in their path."

"And Lou didn't get stung?"

"She didn't complain of it. And anyway, since she keeps bees, she's probably used to getting stung."

"Sounds like an open and shut case, then," Sam cynically stated. "Is that why she's under house arrest?"

"It's for her comfort as much as anything. We don't really have accommodations for someone her age. Besides, there's a bit of a mob mentality here in Edenton sometimes. She's safe from cruel words and jeers if she stays at home. She's comfortable there. James goes and checks on her every morning, just as he's done for years. He brings her groceries or her medicines, so really, she's getting waited on, hand and foot."

"And how long do you anticipate she's going to have to stay put?"

Well, the service for Harvey is in two days, and then we'll start the trial sometime after that."

"But what's the point?" Sam stood up to leave, deliberately controlling his temper with serious breathing.

"Now, Mr. McClellan, we will be sure she has a fair trial. Her attorney is hard at work on the case. Feel free to visit him if you have further questions." Chief Harris stood up an offered his hand to Sam.

Sam turned around without shaking it and left the chief's office in a huff. He passed James on the way out.

"Can I give you a lift, Sam?" James called.

"No, thanks. I need to walk. Uh, can you tell me who Lou's attorney is, James?"

"Bill Jackson. His office is on Queen Street, just a few blocks up Broad, if you don't mind walking," James smiled. "Turn right after you see the real estate office on the corner, and it's the third building on the right, a little brick building across from the courthouse. And after you finish there, if you keep walking straight on Queen, you'll run right into Oak Street. Turn left, and two houses up, you're back at Lou's. Isn't Edenton great?"

"Yeah, James. It's terrific."

CHAPTER SEVEN

Sam passed several joggers and walkers on his way up Broad Street. After a peek in the street-side garden of the historic Cupola House, Sam walked across King Street toward a two-story granite building that was now the city's municipal building. A hardware store clerk swept the brick-paved sidewalk in front of his store, stopping for Sam to pass and offering a cheerful hello to him. A few shopkeepers were washing huge plate glass windows, opening shutters, or unlocking doors to businesses selling everything from clothing and shoes to gifts and antiques.

One place had two café tables outside, an invitation if Sam ever saw one. Sam's nose picked up the scent of roasting coffee. Sam veered into the Sound Side Acoustic Cafe.

Several card racks and shelf units offered gifts for shoppers, but the real treats were in a glass case resting on a countertop. Pastries, muffins, and slices of different cakes, all individually wrapped, enticed coffee-buyers who stood at the counter, waiting for their brews to be created.

Sam took his place in line behind two chattering women, fresh from a morning walk judging by their short shorts, tank tops, and wind-swept blond hair they both tried to put back in place. When they stopped primping, Sam noticed they both had the same hairstyles and coloring. *Twins?*

A heavyset couple stood off to the side, ogling pastries, debating the merits of each one presented in the tall revolving case. As Sam waited, he scanned the shop. Twelve-foot tin ceilings painted light brown mirrored the floor-to-ceiling bookshelves lined with five-gallon jars of coffee beans and coffee flavorings. In the far corner behind the bar was a huge coffee roaster, sending off rich scents. Fits of steam escaped the espresso machine next to the ubiquitous cold drinks case.

In each of the bay windows on either side of the front door sat two small café tables, complete with red and white checkered tablecloths topped with small glass vases of fresh-looking flowers. Two taller and larger "pub" tables with appropriate-sized chairs clustered on one side of the café. Anchoring the other side of the place was an overstuffed but comfortable-looking coffee-brown couch and matching chair cornering a wide coffee table made of what looked like planks of wood from a weathered barn. Acoustic music Sam didn't recognize drifted softly over small speakers set in the bookcase behind the counter.

A petite woman in a coffee-brown apron did her best to keep the orders flowing. "Welcome to the Sound Side Acoustic Cafe. What can I fix for you?" She rested her hands on the countertop for just a minute before grabbing a towel to wipe it down.

"Black coffee would be great." Sam appreciated her hard work. Maybe he'd stop by again while he was in Edenton. "You the owner?"

"Yep," she called over her shoulder as she finished up with the heavyset couple's order and rung up the cash register. She pulled two juices from a top-loading refrigerator and two slices of chocolate-covered pound cake for the blond walkers. After ringing them up, she moved back to Sam's order. "We bought this place about six years ago, and my husband and I fixed it up."

"Looks great. Where does the 'acoustic' part come from?"

"We have live music in here several times a week, and the local writers' group meets here, too. Sometimes, we have poetry readings, but they aren't quite as popular as the live music."

"How late are you open?" Sam paid for his coffee.

"Just until nine at night. We open at seven o'clock in the morning, so that's a full day for us."

"Well, thanks. This is great. I'll be back." Sam walked toward the door, opening it for a gorgeous brunette entering. He was about to head out, but he stopped in his tracks when he heard the petite coffee mistress call out a hello to the woman walking in the door.

"Monica Maples, I've been waiting for you. You're about five minutes late today…. I was beginning to wonder if I should send the Marines out to find you," she said with a laugh. "Your usual?"

"Marines, Bets? That might have proved interesting. I like a man in uniform," Miss Maples answered teasingly as she leaned on the counter. "I had an early morning appointment in Edenton Bay Plantation, and the security gate was slow to open on my way out of the property. Another listing in there—right on the water. It's a fabulous place, too. I'm sure it won't take any time to sell."

Sam watched as the two women gabbed like long-time friends. Closing the café door, Sam slid back inside. He took a seat at one of the empty café tables in the window. While he waited for Monica, he surveyed every exposed inch of her. There was a lot to see: three-inch spiked cherry-red heels accentuated shapely, tanned calves; legs that didn't want to stop even up in the short red skirt; a sculptured jacket with embroidered tulips cascading off of it; lipstick that matched her suit perfectly; and thick sun-streaked brown hair flowing free to the middle of her back. Sam guessed her to be in her mid- to late-thirties, but well-preserved at any age.

Sam watched as Monica looked in the pastry cabinet. "Bets, I'll have a piece of the pound cake, today. It looks luscious."

Sam couldn't agree more.

After she paid her tab, Monica swished back toward the door, juggling purse, wallet, and a small tan bag of pound cake and coffee.

"Need some help?" Sam called, half-standing from his seat.

"Oh, thanks. I just need to put the coffee down for a minute while I put my wallet back." Monica placed her cup on the table, then the pound cake, and focused on returning her bulging wallet to a small red purse shaped like a tulip.

"As long as you're here, why not have a seat and stay a while?" Sam beamed, holding a chair out for her.

"Well, aren't you the gentleman? A little early for a pick-up line, don't you think?" She smiled like a cat about to pounce on a mouse.

"Depends on what you consider early." Sam put out his hand and smiled. "Sam McClellan, at your service."

Monica laughed, held out her hand, and took the offered seat. "Pleased to meet you, Sam McClellan. Monica Maples. You new in town? I think I would have remembered seeing you around before."

"Just in town long enough to fix the engine on my boat. Seems like a great place. Have you lived here long?"

"Not too long. I moved here from Charlotte. What kind of engine trouble do you have?" Monica leaned her elbows on the table, giving the white tank top a chance to reveal a little of what it barely contained.

"Not sure, exactly. But I'm off to find a mechanic today to sort it out. How about you?"

"I don't have any engine trouble," Monica laughed. "But I do need to get to work. I have a client coming in at nine this morning for a tour."

"Care to give me a tour later?" Sam hedged.

"If you are in the market, sure," said Monica, flirting back. "My real estate office is at the corner of Queen and Broad. I get off at six today, if you'd care for an early supper. Let's say seven o'clock?" Monica got up to leave, gathering her purse, bag of cake, and coffee.

"I'll walk with you, if you don't mind. Then you can give me the abbreviated narrative of downtown for starters. And I'll leave it to you to select tonight's restaurant." Sam held the door open for her and followed her out.

"We'll just go to Waterman's Grill. It's over there," she said, nodding to the restaurant with the tugboat on top. "It's been here a long time. I've been told there have been some really good restaurants in Edenton, but even since I moved here, two have gone out of business. For one reason or another, they don't have…staying power." Monica quickly assessed Sam from head to toe, and smiled a brilliant smile.

Sam returned the visual assessment as they walked up the one block to Monica's office. Then they stood face to face. "I look forward to seeing you again," said Sam, offering his hand.

"As do I, Sam. Thank you for the escort." Monica lightly shook Sam's hand. "I appreciate the company. See you at six." She turned and entered the office.

Sam watched her take a seat at a desk near the window and wave to him. He returned the wave. Then he walked down Queen Street until he found Bill Jackson's office, just as James had described it.

CHAPTER EIGHT

"Sam McClellan here to see Bill Jackson," said Sam, introducing himself to the round receptionist with a bee-hive hairstyle as he entered the small but well-appointed waiting room.

Leather-clad wing chairs surrounded a glass top coffee table that clearly showed the Oriental rug underneath. Prints of duck decoys and wet retrievers with limp ducks hung on golden-hued walls, all in matching mats and mahogany frames. A stuffed mallard took its last flight on the spit of wall over the door. A dog-eared stack of *Hunting World* magazines found homes on top of the glass table, the two side tables, and a bookshelf near the receptionist's desk. It appeared that if Bill Jackson wasn't setting someone up for a kill or getting someone off the hook, he was hunting. *If only the aft rail-sitting Kathy could meet Bill Jackson*, Sam thought. Maybe Bill would like a present before Sam left Edenton. Sam would be happy to oblige.

The door to the back area buzzed, and a well-dressed slim man in his late sixties entered the reception area. His tie was the color of pumpkin soup, and his hair, what there was of it, was silver. He approached Sam with a smile and an outstretched hand.

"Mr. McClellan," he bellowed for a non-apparent audience, "I'm Bill Jackson. Welcome to my office. Won't you please follow me? In here," he said, pointing to a conference room lined with law books. "Mabel, hold my calls, will you, dear?"

"Yes, sir, Mr. Jackson." Not once did the receptionist's eyes leave her *Reader's Digest* magazine.

"Need a coffee?" Mr. Jackson offered.

"No thanks; I've just had some. Mr. Jackson, you act as if you were expecting me."

"Indeed. I got a call earlier this morning from the police station telling me you were on your way. I didn't expect the walk would take you quite this long." Mr. Jackson grinned.

"I stopped for coffee and was talking up a local about the area." Sam sat down in a plush chair. He tried to tip it back as was his custom. No such luck in this chair.

"Ah. And you may call me Bill. May I call you Sam?"

"Sure, Bill. I'm hoping you can shed some light on what's going on with my aunt's case. Seems the whole town thinks she's guilty."

"Yes, I've heard as much. But we don't suspect such a thing, do we?" Bill sat down in a chair, mirroring Sam's posture and tone.

"What do *we* know so far about the incident?" Sam ignored the rhetorical question.

"We know that Mr. Harvey Bishop, who was a businessman and a friend to many in this town, died late one night." Bill sounded like he was practicing his opening lines for a jury and judge. Maybe he always sounded that way. "Four nights ago, to be precise. We know he was in relatively good health for a man his age, according to his physician. An autopsy was performed, and it appears he died from anaphylactic shock from a series of stings. We know there were no signs of forced entry. We also know there were no signs of wasp nests in or under his home. We know there were no fingerprints found that were unexpected. And as a point of fact, the most common ones we found, other than Harvey's, belonged to your dear aunt, my good friend and client, Lou McClellan."

"Well, they were friends," Sam broke the monologue. "Such good friends, in fact, that they were planning to be married. Do you think she'd seek to kill a man she was about to marry?"

"Ah, yes. The marriage proposal," Bill sat back, slowly crossing his arms for effect. "There *is* that. The very day that a conversation about such a marriage occurred, Harvey was in here asking me to change his will."

"And that wasn't a conflict of interest, for you to be lawyer to both suspect and victim?"

"Well, he wasn't a victim until he died. And he may not have been a victim of foul play, as it stands. It may have been accidental, with an errant bee or ten somehow entering his room and stinging him. I defer to the police for their brilliant deduction capabilities on that matter. I was, however, attorney to both Mr. Bishop and Miss McClellan long before this occurred, so until we determine that there was indeed a crime and the matter goes to trial, I see no point in assuming that I am not the counsel for Lou."

"Okay," said Sam, "so let's assume for the moment that you are still the attorney for both parties. Tell me about the will."

"As I understand it, Mr. McClellan, you are a suspect's nephew, and that does not entitle you to confidential information."

"Okay, so there was a change in the will. Has it been read?"

"No. That will happen after the service the day after tomorrow. I am sure you are welcome to come as your aunt's guest and escort. She is named in the will, after all."

"Thanks, I'll be there. Are you the only one who knows what's in Harvey's will?"

"Yes. It is a confidential matter to make one's will." Bill leaned over the table, lowering his voice. "Have you considered writing a will for yourself? You never know when death will come knocking on your door. I could see you later this afternoon to help you plan your estate, if you like."

"Thanks, Mr. Jackson, but I think I'm covered in that respect." Sam rolled his chair back and stood. "I'll see you the day after tomorrow, Mr. Jackson. Thanks for your time."

"Anytime, my good man. Anytime." Mr. Jackson thrust out his hand to Sam.

Sam shook it, feeling he would need to wash his hands within the next two minutes.

CHAPTER NINE

Once out of Bill Jackson's office, Sam turned to his right and walked the short block to Oak Street, then left on Oak toward Lou's house. Stepping on the porch, Sam heard the television in the front room, Lou's bedroom.

"Hello, Aunt Lou," Sam called so as not to startle her as he opened the front door to the foyer. No response. Sam tapped lightly on her door, which was closed to the foyer. Still no response. When Sam knocked hard on the door, a flushed Lou swung it open wide.

"What is the matter, Sammy?"

Sam took one look at his towel-draped, dripping great-aunt and apologized profusely. "I'm so sorry to disturb you, Aunt Lou. I just got nervous when I didn't hear you."

"I'm fine, Sam. Just needed a little soak in the tub. Now, what can I help you with?" Lou didn't move from the doorway.

"I just wanted to borrow the car and get directions to the mechanic's shop." Sam blushed.

"The keys are on the table by the door. I wrote down the directions for you in case you came back while I was…indisposed. Lunch is at noon, and I'll expect you here." With that, she closed the door to her bedroom.

Sam found the keys and directions to Al's on the front hall table and slunk out.

It was a short drive to the mechanic's shop, and judging by the looks of the area, Sam bet that not many tourists got to see this side of Edenton. Shotgun houses with overgrown lots punctuated by rusted out cars on cinderblocks lined both sides of the street. An occasional business popped up, with bars on windows, suggesting the nefarious nature of this side of town. Sam found the address he was looking for and turned his aunt's car into the crushed marl driveway between two twelve-foot high barbed wire fences. *Nice place*, he thought.

Ahead was a small red building with a large plate glass window overlooking the yard. Sam parked as close to it as he could. As he stepped out of the car, a huge Rottweiler bounded toward him, teeth bared. Sam quickly calculated the distance between him and the dog, and him and the door, and dashed for the door.

Once inside, Sam breathed. The low-ceiling held down a fog of cigar smoke. Sam squinted to see a man entering the office from a bay located on the opposite wall, cigar hanging from his mouth. A wreath of smoke encircled his bald head.

"Help you?" the cigar-chomping man called.

"I'm having some difficulty with my boat engine. I think it might be the fuel pump, and I wonder if you can help me." Sam held his breath. The stink of the place reminded him of his former police partner, Lee. The memory of his partner's murder rose to the forefront of Sam's brain. He had to shake it off and focus on the cigar chomper in front of him.

"What kinda engine?" Cigar Chomper leaned to his right. "That your car?"

"No, I borrowed it from my aunt."

"I recognize it. Worked on it many a time. Too bad. She was a good customer." Cigar Chomper walked back into the bay without further ado.

"What do you mean?" Sam took two steps to follow him.

"Can't do no work for any relation to a murderer." Cigar Chomper returned to his mat on the bay's floor under a pale yellow Mercedes. "It's against my principles."

"If you had any principles, you'd not hang an innocent woman until her guilt is established." Sam walked out of the bay before Cigar Chomper could answer. His pet was sitting patiently outside.

"Nice doggie," Sam whispered, slowing his walk.

The dog growled and stood up in a crouched position. There were those teeth again.

"Nice doggie," Sam repeated as he whipped open the passenger's side door and crawled into the driver's seat. Gunning it, Sam fishtailed out of the yard's lot, nearly hitting the dog.

The dog stopped at the fence, barking for all of Edenton to hear.

Sam found his way to Broad Street, the main road into town, and headed the other way. He passed a hospital, a grocery store, gas stations, and fast food joints—all the necessary businesses that had no place within the confines of the postcard-perfect waterfront historic district.

The road eventually found open expanses of fields filled with corn and peanuts, remnants of cotton balls still on their stalks, and other crops Sam couldn't name. Large clapboard-sided farmhouses stood close to the road. Some were in desperate need of repair, while others looked like they'd be perfect backdrops for a movie about another time. Pecan trees seemed to be everywhere Sam looked, adding to the beauty of the flat county.

Sam fished around in the glove compartment for a map. Auntie didn't disappoint. There was a state map as well as a county map. On the county map was a highlighted road—the one Sam was on—and a turn off to the left heading toward the Chowan River. Bingo.

Sam followed the main road for another few miles, then marked the turnoff road with his finger. River Way. "There it is." Sam saw the tattered road sign on his left. The post leaned dangerously close to the ground.

Ahead was more farmland for about two miles. Then the road curved sharply to the right. Asphalt pavement gave way to gravel, which soon gave way to a narrow rutted dirt road. There on the left was a dilapidated wooden structure, standing right on the banks of the Chowan River. Sam slowed down and pulled into the well-worn parking area bordered by logs silver with age. The sign on the building told him he was in the right place: Bishop's Fishery.

The building had seen better days, with fogged windows (some of the panes were missing), man-sized exhaust vents nearly falling out of their frames on the building's walls, and paint chipping off of the Chinese red door. Sam walked slowly around the building. Carefully hoisting himself up on the lopsided loading dock that jutted out into the river a few feet, Sam immediately saw the appeal to a developer. The wide waters of the Chowan River ran fast by here, but there was a silt island just a few feet away from the dock's edge. A perfect setting on a gorgeous river. Sam could imagine a gazebo out on that island, or a restaurant with waterside dining and tie-ups for transient boaters. Clearly, this site was worth millions, despite its occupant's current condition.

Sam circled back to the front of the ivy-choked building, noting more broken panes of glass. He felt someone's
stare boring through his back as he got back into the car.
Out of habit, Sam kept one eye on the rearview mirror as
he drove back to town.

CHAPTER TEN

"I need your help." It was a simple request, but it was one Sam felt odd asking into his cellphone.

The voice on the other end was enthusiastic. "Sam! I'm so glad to hear from you! Are you in trouble again? Where are you?"

"I'm in Edenton, and my engine died. I think it's the fuel pump. Do you know how to repair it, Molly?"

"Piece of cake, if you're sure that's what it is, Dude. Tell me what happened, what you heard. And tell me about your engine."

Molly Monroe knew her engines. She ought to. She had two of them on her classic motorboat that she'd restored. Unfortunately, Sam knew she would have to restore it all again, and Sam felt guilty about it. While she had been helping him with a case involving drug trafficking around the resort island of Bald Head and through small beach communities, Molly lost her boat—and nearly her life—because of poor choices Sam made. He'd never forget what he put her through, or how she helped him before.

Sam replayed *Angel's* engine's last moments and gave her the particulars of the motor.

Molly, in turn, told him what to order. "I'll be up in a day or so when the part comes in. I'll help you install the fuel pump. It's going to take about a day, but we can do it."

"You've done this before, I take it?" Sam was delighted to hear Molly's voice, and even more pleased she was willing to come to Edenton, given how their last night together in Carolina Beach ended before he left town.

"Sure. They go out from time to time, and I've had to replace one on my engines at least once or twice. We'll figure it out. Where can I find you?"

"I'm staying with my aunt here in Edenton. Got something to write on? I'll give you the address."

Sam gave her directions to Lou's.

"I'll drive your car, if you don't mind. It needs some exercise."

"That's fine. I knew I could count on you. And Molly?"

"Yes, Sam?"

"This time, I promise no sinking boats."

Molly laughed. "The only one I care about has been raised, Sam. You'll be glad to hear she's pumped dry as of yesterday, and I've started ripping out the galley. It's a real mess, but I have plans to improve her layout a bit."

"Sorry you're having to do that, Mol. Maybe after I visit my son, I can help you. I feel I need to help, after all we went through."

"Ah, we can talk about it later." Molly sounded rushed. "I've got to go. Time to dock."

"Dock? Where are you?"

"Boat delivery from Barbados, just ahead of a storm. I'll be up there in a day or so. See ya."

Sam looked at the phone in his hand. "See ya." Sam was sitting in Lou's driveway, wondering whether Lou was out of her bath yet.

Approaching the front door, Sam noted a screen in one of the windows needed repair. Checking two others on that level, he saw a few more tears that could be easily fixed. *A good afternoon project.*

Lunch was indeed ready, as Lou promised. After they ate, Sam poked around in the shed until he found an amount of rubber spline and left-over screening material. He managed to fix three screens before running out of materials. Aunt Lou sat nearby and told Sam about Edenton's history. He's heard it all before, but it was still nice to spend time with her this way.

CHAPTER ELEVEN

Looking in the mirror one last time, Sam smoothed his black hair into place. He'd borrowed an iron from Aunt Lou for his short-sleeve copper-checked shirt, then decided against it and chosen a white cable-knit sweater to go with his jeans. Flip-flops didn't seem appropriate, but that's what he had with him, so they would have to do for his dinner date with Monica Maples. The smell of porkchops and onions wafted up the stairs, pulling Sam downstairs and into the kitchen. It wasn't until he was halfway into the kitchen he realized he was hungry again. Good thing. Sam felt obliged to eat with Lou before meeting Monica this evening.

"Oh, wow. That smells great!"

"Thank you, Sammy. I've got everything just about ready." Lou decorated a plate of oven-baked porkchops with a small garnish of parsley on top of sliced tomatoes. She handed it to Sam. "Take this and put it on the trivet in the dining room, would you? I'll bring the rice. The rest is in there already."

Sam obeyed and sat down with Lou to the dinner. He'd forgotten to tell her he was going out, but since it was only five-thirty, Lou's usual dinner hour, he felt obliged to stay and eat with her. When he bit into a porkchop, he was pleased with his obligation.

"Perfect."

"Glad you like it. I make a big batch and freeze what I don't eat so I can enjoy the leftovers whenever I make this dish. You can help yourself if you get hungry later on."

"I doubt I'll be hungry later on. In fact, I'm going to have to walk this off tonight." Sam was being honest.

"That's fine. Just let yourself in and lock up behind you."

"Aunt Lou, what do you know about Harvey's daughter?" Sam changed the subject.

"I never met her. I was so upset to learn about her that I didn't want to meet her. I know that may sound petty, but it is how I felt. Since Harvey's death, well, I've just not had the heart to seek her out. I really don't see the point. All I know about her is what I've already told you, and that was only what Harvey told me about her. Why do you ask?"

"Well, I did some checking around today. Her name didn't come up, except for a conversation I had with your lawyer."

"Well, that's not unusual. Around here, locals don't pay too much attention to outsiders. It's always been that way. I suppose she'll be at the funeral?"

"I suppose so," Sam replied with a full mouth. "I will be with you, though, if you want to go."

"I haven't decided if I'm going. What do you think?"

"It's better for you to go. Otherwise, it looks like you have something to hide, which I know you don't."

"I'll think about it." Lou got up from the table and started to clear away the plates. "I think we'll eat in the dining room here while you're visiting. It's so much more civilized than eating at the bar, don't you agree?"

"Whatever you want is fine with me, Aunt Lou. That was a wonderful meal. Thank you." Sam followed her into the kitchen, but he was admonished when he tried to cross its threshold.

"You're welcome, Sammy," Lou said. "Now you run along. I have a system, remember?"

"Yes, I remember. I'll see you later." Sam left Lou to do her system, whatever that meant.

The walk back to Monica's real estate office was short. The clear evening sky was streaked with plumes of orange over pale blue. *Red sky at night, sailor's delight,* Sam thought. Tomorrow would be a good day to work on the boat. Earlier in the day he had called around to a few places in Elizabeth City to order the parts Molly wanted him to get, but he thought he'd go aboard the boat tomorrow to change the oil filter and do a few other needed chores until Molly arrived. Elizabeth City was a short forty-five minute drive north of Edenton, and if everything worked the way he hoped, he and Molly could drive there to pick up his order when she arrived in town.

Monica was seated at her window-side desk, cradling a phone in one hand and writing with the other when Sam walked by her office.

Monica waved and motioned for him to come inside when she saw him.

Sam waited for her in the vestibule of the old brick building. A huge bulletin board was covered with pictures and information sheets of various properties and the occasional motorboat, all with eye-popping price tags.

"Hope I haven't kept you waiting," said Monica, sashaying toward him.

"Not at all. I thought I was late."

"Just as well. I was on the phone. The phone rarely rests in my job. Ready for supper?"

Sam smiled. "Sure. I'm ready to eat." He thought of his aunt's porkchops, the taste still in his mouth. He offered his arm to Monica.

"Why, thank you," Monica giggled as she accepted and slipped her arm through his. "I've been in and out of the office all day, and I'm starving."

Together, they strolled down two blocks toward the waterfront and stepped into the Waterman's Grill. In front of them stood a deli counter filled with gourmet cheeses. Wine lined either side of the small entrance room, and gift baskets sat high on shelves.

The young hostess put down a phone receiver and greeted them. "Hey! Two for dinner?"

Sam and Monica followed the petite girl in a light blue sweater dress through the filled-to-capacity seating area in the bar and up a flight of mahogany stairs. Exposed red brick surrounded the window-lined room filled with twice as many tables as downstairs. Half of the tables were full. The hostess drifted toward a window table, lit a tiny votive, and placed menus on the plank table.

Sam helped Monica into her seat, then sat himself. Monica looked radiant, and he drank her in like a cool glass of water.

"Tell me what's good here." Sam drew his eyes toward the menu.

"Most everything. I'm famished."

A waitress bopped over, pony-tail swinging as she bounced. "Hi. My name is Sheila. Can I get you a drink?"

"Chardonnay for me," said Monica, not hesitating.

"What's on draft?" Sam noted the baby bump under Sheila's tight white T-shirt.

Sheila listed Sam's choices, never once making eye contact.

"I'll have a Bud, please."

Sheila bounced away to get their drinks.

"So tell me about yourself, Sam." Monica leaned her elbows on the table, slowly clasped her hands under her chin, and waited.

"Uh, I sailed in to Edenton, my engine quit, and I'm trying to get it repaired before sailing off. That what you had in mind?" Sam tipped his chair back to the point of falling and balanced himself.

"That's a good start. Where did you come from? And where are you going? How long will you be here, and tell me about your…aunt, I think you said this morning?"

"From Carolina Beach to Norfolk, don't know how long it will take to fix the engine, and my aunt has lived here as long as I can remember. How about you?"

"From Charlotte, moved here three months ago, hooked up with a local real estate company so that I could continue to work, and I don't know where I'm going next." Monica didn't move her pose, even when Sheila bounced back with drinks.

"Ready to order?"

Sheila was about eighteen, Sam guessed. She wouldn't be turning tables too much longer judging from the size of her belly.

"I'll have the lump crabmeat dish and a spinach salad," Monica said without looking at her menu again.

"Sounds good. Make it two," Sam said to make it easy on Sheila.

Sheila grabbed the menus and bounced away without a word.

"You're leaving, too? After just three months? What's the matter—not enough excitement for you here?"

"Actually, a little too much." Monica cupped her wine-glass and stared into it like it was a crystal ball. "I came in search of something, and it's not here."

Sam wasn't sure whether this was mourning or not, so he pressed on. "What something?"

"A relationship I never had. But as it turns out, it wasn't that important after all."

"Important to you? Or to the other person?"

"The other person, apparently. My father, to be specific."

"Your father was here?"

"Yes. I barely knew the man. We were on good terms when he got over his initial shock. He didn't know about me all these years. I, on the other hand, well, I had a quest to find him all my growing up years."

"And finding the Holy Grail wasn't what you expected?"

"It was a bit of a letdown, actually. He didn't like being dragged into the past, I guess."

"You want to talk about it?"

"Well, I really shouldn't get into it." Monica smiled, then proceeded. "He and my mother met forty years ago. The way my mother told the story, it was a wild trip to the beach, to Nags Head, when she was in her hippie days. She was a little older than I am, I guess. She met him there. They hit it off, and before she knew it, my mom was spending all her time with him. It was just a few days full of parties, but it was the nights that mattered, according to Mother. She wanted desperately to continue seeing him, but he wasn't interested. Said he had too busy a life to include a woman at that point. Too complicated. Too busy with work, running his business, etc., he told her." Monica sat upright.

"So my mother never told him she got pregnant during that trip to the beach, and they went on about their lives. My mom returned to Charlotte, eventually settled down, and raised me with the help of her begrudging parents. We never saw or heard from Harvey."

"Harvey?"

"Harvey Bishop. My father."

"And so he's what brought you to Edenton?"

"Yes. About five years ago, my mother passed away. On her deathbed, she revealed his name to me for the first time. Seeing that he was once someone special to my mom, I somehow felt obliged to track him down and tell him the news."

"How did he take it?"

"At first, he was in utter shock. Not so much about my mother passing away; I guess that comes with the love 'em and leave 'em territory. Maybe the thought of immortality affected him funny when confronted with his past; I don't know. He seemed genuinely upset, though, that he hadn't been part of *my* life all these years. Eventually, he welcomed me into his home and into his life. He told me his side of the story of his affair with my mother, or what he could remember of it, anyway. It was a drunken time for both of them, but he didn't remember her calling him afterward—in fact, he remembered it being quite the opposite. He said he called on her, and she said she didn't want to see him. He was from a lower class than she was, and it mattered greatly in her family. Harvey told me he felt defeated, but still he persisted and continued to write her letters and call her. He said she still refused to see him. Then she wrote a letter stating that she was getting married, so he left her alone. Of course, that was a long time ago. My mother never told me of any letters, so Harvey had no proof of his devotion."

"Did your mother marry?"

"No. She raised me alone and worked herself to death to see that I had a good shot at life."

Sheila bounced back to the table, carrying identical plates. She did her job of placing them efficiently on the table, then bounced away.

"Tell me about your relationship with Harvey." Sam dove into the lump crab. It was just as advertised, no filling, just meat.

"Well, we got acquainted over dinners, and everything was fine. Until four days ago."

"What happened?"

"He died a horrible death. He was stung by bees or wasps; I can't tell the difference. Murdered in his own bed by his longtime friend, the story goes. Haven't you picked up a paper?"

"I just got here yesterday. But I'm learning a lot without reading a paper. I have a confession, Monica."

Monica stopped eating and stared at Sam. "Already? We just met."

"My aunt is your father's neighbor. She told me a bit about what happened. She's Lou McClellan. I didn't know any of this had happened until I got here."

Monica slowly put down her fork. "Of course. Your last name and hers…McClellan. I feel like I'm having dinner with the enemy." Monica glared at Sam.

"I'm not the enemy, and neither is my aunt, until she is proven guilty. Can't we sort this thing out together?"

"Word is she did it because of me. She couldn't stand the thought that he had a child out of wedlock."

"If we could, let's wait and see what the evidence proves." Sam tried his best to restore the evening. "How about dessert?"

"Another glass of wine will be my dessert." Monica regained her composure and smiled.

Sam flagged Sheila for the order and finished his crab dish. With salads left mostly untouched, Sheila cleared the table when she brought round two of drinks.

"Hello, Monica." A tall blond man barreled up to the table, looking like he had just walked off a rugby field.

"Hi, Paul. Paul, this is Sam. Sam, this is Paul Shepherd."

Paul thrust out his burly hand to Sam. "Nice to meet you," he said through his teeth. Paul's eyes never left Monica, though he still spoke to Sam. "In town for long?"

"No, just long enough to fix the engine on my sailboat. Monica was kind enough to show me around town a little."

"Monica's kind, all right. Enjoy your visit." Then to Monica, Paul said with a tad more sweetness in his voice, "See you Saturday?"

Monica ignored his leer. "Sure, Paul. I'll be there." She waved him off, and he obeyed. His eyes never left her, even as he walked back down the stairs.

"Didn't mean to stir the pot," Sam started.

"Oh, Paul's always stirred up about something. He usually comes here after work to drink downstairs with his buddies. Sheila must have told him I was here. Edenton's small, remember. It's hard not to know other people's business." Monica nearly finished her wine in one gulp. "About ready to go?" She placed fifty dollars on the table and stood up to leave.

"This is my treat." Sam tried to give her the money back, but his efforts fell on deaf ears.

Monica was already heading for the stairs.

Sam hurried to catch up with her and followed her outside into the cooling evening air.

"I baked a pumpkin pie yesterday," said Monica, sashaying along. "Come have a piece with me." Monica walked briskly toward the waterfront, then turned right in front of the police station.

Sam caught up with her. "I thought you said the second glass of wine was dessert."

"Well, my dessert's better. Promise." There was that teasing lilt in her voice, again—the one Sam had heard earlier in the cafe.

The two walked past the park, following the curve in the street until it crossed King Street. Turning left on King away from town, Monica stopped long enough to take off her high heels. "That's enough of those."

"Will you stay in Edenton?" Sam walked beside Monica on the narrow sidewalk, ducking the occasional drape of a low-hanging branch of golden yellow and green willow leaves.

"I don't know," Monica sighed. "It's a nice town and all, but there's no reason for me to stay. I have a few matters to clear up, what with Harvey…Dad passing on, and I suppose after that's all over with, I'll move on, or perhaps I'll go back to Charlotte. With my real estate license, I can pretty much cozy up to whatever agency I want. I'm good at sales, so it's not hard to walk right into a place." Turning down one more street, Monica stopped at the base of a driveway running between a Presbyterian church and a small cedar-shingled cottage with butter-colored shutters. "This is home for the time being. It's small, but it suits my needs."

Sam followed her up the driveway and onto a covered porch on the side of the house. A picket fence surrounded the backyard, while drooping crape myrtles filled the well-groomed front yard with hot pink blossoms. Everywhere there were small garden vignettes filled with hydrangeas or irises or wild violets. On the porch was a table surrounded by four cushy chairs. Two long green matchstick blinds hung from the porch's ceiling, making the otherwise open-air porch seem cozy and private. The wall closest to the glass French door into the house was brick. *The back of a fireplace*, thought Sam. It was the perfect dry spot for the stacked fire-wood that filled the nook between fireplace wall and door.

"Come on in," Monica purred. "It's a cozy little cottage." Monica felt around the base of a Tiffany-style lamp for the switch. The soft light glowed pink through the stain-glass shade, its long edges dripping like a weeping willow. "I was lucky to get it. According to many, this place is a favor-ite rental in town. If you ask around long enough, you'll learn most everyone in town has rented it at one time or another. Seems it's irresistible. I found out who owned it, approached him with an offer, and it's mine. I didn't expect to buy something, but I couldn't resist it either."

"And when you leave?"

"I'll keep it rented. I know it won't be a problem."

When Sam stepped inside, he saw the cottage's charm. To his right, cream-colored floor-to-ceiling bookcases surrounded an oversized window. The walls were painted a warm cinnamon color, and the trim was off-white. To his left was a small eating area, and beyond that, a separate kitchen complete with porcelain sink and tiles on the walls. In front of him was a huge colorful fish tank with a bedroom door on either side of it. In one room, he could see the edge of a bed. The other, straight ahead, was filled with a grand desk and bookcases. The fireplace was filled to capacity with an old wood-burning stove. Most likely, it could warm the entire cottage. A pale green and cream-striped sofa sat parallel to the fireplace, and two inviting chairs abutted a well-used coffee table. The arrangement begged for company to linger over drinks, and to become cozy and intimate, like the rest of the cottage.

"Nine hundred square feet?" Sam guessed.

"Seven hundred and twenty, actually. But it's still a palace compared to being on a boat, I'll bet." Monica threw her shoes and purse on her bed and took off her petal-strewn jacket. She walked into the kitchen, then motioned for Sam to follow her. She turned on a small teapot-shaped lamp.

"Palatial. Yes. It's wonderful. Better than that, it's perfect."

"You want perfect? Wait until you taste this." Monica busied herself with Depression-era green glass plates, cloth napkins, and a deep-dish pumpkin pie. "Grab some glasses out of that cupboard. No, not that one; the one over next to the sink." With her elbow, she pointed toward a cream-colored cabinet with ancient black hinges that creaked when he opened the door.

Sam found more plates and a shelf full of decorative wineglasses. He pulled two out and set them on the green tile counter, awaiting further instructions. He didn't have to wait long.

"I saw you had a beer, but all I have is wine. The corkscrew is in that drawer to your left. Be a dear and get a bottle out of the fridge."

Sam obeyed. With full glasses in hand, he followed Monica back to the living room. He watched her place plates, forks, and matching cloth napkins on the coffee table in front of the sofa, then flop down in front of the cozy arrangement. Sam handed Monica a glass. Before he could sit down in one of the opposing chairs, she patted the sofa beside her.

"Don't be shy, Sam. Come sit here." Monica moved slightly on the sofa, making very little more room for Sam.

Sam sat down next to her and started in on the pie. He waited for her to join him, but her plate never left the table.

Before Sam finished his dessert, Monica moved a little closer, close enough to smell. A faint scent of jasmine rose from her skin. Sam leaned back and looked at the fish tank on the wall behind the sofa.

"Nice collection. Where did you get them all?" Sam tried to divert her attention.

"Various places." Monica didn't look away from him. "Many of them came from the Great Barrier Reef. Lovely creatures, aren't they?"

"Uh, yeah." Sam felt her hand on his thigh. He moved his leg slightly, and when Monica didn't move her hand, he stood up and walked toward the aquarium. Its contents included several brightly-hued fish of various kinds and a drab-looking, brownish-yellow octopus about the size of a golf ball.

"Did you pick them out yourself?" He heard Monica's wineglass touch the coffee table.

"I did. Diving is a hobby of mine. Australia has fabulous spots. Ever tried it?" Monica slid up beside Sam in front of the aquarium.

"Once, but it was a long time ago. I think I prefer being topside." It'd been a long time since he was nervous with a woman, but Sam felt jittery.

"Funny. I like being on top, too." Monica didn't waste time. She melted into the space between Sam and the tank, wrapped her arms around his back, and pulled him in tight. "Want to take this into the other room?" She stood on her toes and kissed Sam hard on the lips.

"Mon…i…ca…," said Sam, trying to talk between her lip bites. "I don't think this is a good…idea." He couldn't believe what had just come out of his mouth. She was hot and ready. Maybe that's what bothered him.

"Why not, Sam?" Monica backed off a little, standing flat-footed. She pressed her pelvis against Sam and wiggled a little. "We're both adults."

"What about Paul? Isn't he…."

"Paul's just Paul. We were seeing each other when I first moved to town, but I broke it off." Monica was rooted to her spot in front of Sam. A smile flickered to her lips.

Sam didn't want to feel the rise in his jeans, but there it was. He couldn't hide it from her, either. He felt her grinding harder, making things worse.

"You said at the restaurant you'd see Paul on Saturday. Sounds to me like you're still seeing him." Sam kissed Monica on the neck. His hands found the ends of her camisole and lifted it out of her skirt.

"There's a sailboat race." Monica's breath quickened. "I'm his crew. It's the last race of the season, and I promised I'd be there. That's all. Besides, there'll be three others on board with us." Monica steered Sam backward toward the darkened bedroom. "Perhaps you'd like a little race?"

"My boat's so loaded, I'd lose, for sure." Sam hesitated. Images of falling back on the bed and pulling Monica along with him flashed in front of him. For a split second, he considered his options: stay and let things take their course, or leave the cottage—and the temptation—immediately. She was moving way too fast for his tastes. Sam started to pull away. "Monica, I…don't think…."

"Hmm?" She took little notice of his hesitation and started to wriggle out of her skirt, one hand still on his chest. "No need. I'll do all the thinking for us." She started undoing her shirt, one button at a time. It seemed to Sam she was well-practiced at this maneuvering, which made the temptation lessen.

Sam tried again. "Monica, I can't. I can't do this with you."

Monica paused, her look like that of a panther summing up a prospective dinner. "Is this a matter of *can't*…?" She kissed him hard on the lips and slid her hand to his crotch. "*That* doesn't seem to be the problem. Perhaps this is a matter of *won't?*"

"It's a little of both," Sam uttered softly, pushing her hand away. "There's someone else in my life, and this wouldn't be right."

"I see." Monica held her ground. "That's a shame. I was hoping you and I could have some fun for a while. Are you sure you won't change your mind? We could be discreet while you're in town—you know, when you sail away, you can pretend like nothing ever happened." Again, Monica leaned close so Sam could feel her hot body next to his.

"That's a lovely invitation, Monica, but I just think it's best for us not to get things…started."

"A little too late for that, don't you think?" Monica wrapped her arms around Sam's neck and tried to pull him to her bed.

"No, I...ah, I'm sorry." Sam gently extracted himself from her arms and stepped away. "I'll let myself out." Sam backed out of the bedroom and headed hurriedly through the kitchen to the back door. Once outside, he fought off the rising lump in his throat and the urge to run. Something wasn't right with him, Sam knew. Here was a magnificent woman, and he was walking—quickly, no less—away.

Halfway back across town to Aunt Lou's, Sam realized why: Molly.

CHAPTER TWELVE

"Thanks, Aunt Lou." Grateful for the coffee, Sam dragged himself to the kitchen island stool.

"You're welcome. And you were awfully late getting home last night."

"Sorry; didn't mean to wake you."

"Oh, you didn't, Sammy. I nap sometimes during the day, and it makes it hard for me to sleep at night. I was reading when I heard you come in."

"Do you always have trouble sleeping?" Sam's head pounded from either too little sleep or too much alcohol.

"Oh, it's been like this for years. I've read a good number of books, though." Lou smiled as she slid a plate of blueberry coffeecake and grapes toward Sam. "I got used to it about nine years ago. I just try to make the best use of the time."

"So you go to bed early, then wake up about when?" Sam hated to sound like a cop investigating a suspect, but the questions just kept coming.

"Usually about two-thirty or three in the morning. I can usually fall back asleep by five. I get up an hour or so later feeling refreshed."

"The night Harvey died…did you have trouble sleeping that night, too?"

"Well, it happens like that every night. Of course, I was awake at the time of his death, based on what James has told me."

"Sorry to bother you about it, Aunt Lou. I just wondered if you had heard anything out of the ordinary that night. Can you think of anything?"

"Not that night, no. But the next morning, one of the trays in my hive was out of alignment. I set it back when I saw it so as not to disturb my bees too much. They get riled when things aren't the way they're supposed to be."

"I know absolutely nothing about bees or their hives. Do you mind showing me what it looked like?" Sam was on his feet, coffee mug in hand.

"Well, I'd be delighted to. I tried to show good ol' James the next morning when he came over, but he was more interested in another helping of strudel." Aunt Lou smiled as she wrapped an oatmeal-colored cardigan around her shoulders and shuffled through the enclosed porch to the back door.

The sight of a stacked washer and dryer unit in a corner of the full pantry on the porch reminded Sam of a long-overdue chore. He'd have to get to his own laundry soon, and he made a mental note to bring what he had from the boat later that day.

A damp blast of humidity greeted Sam as he stepped down the four stairs to a brick patio. Blue sky overhead promised heat for the day. Sam really needed some rain to wash off the boat and, hopefully, chase Kathy away.

"Uh, don't you have to wear something to keep the bees from stinging you?" Sam followed Lou across the neatly trimmed grass toward three short, white wooden boxes in the corner. Nearby flowerbeds barely contained their contents, where budding flowers overflowed well-marked boundaries. Bees buzzed throughout the remains of a vegetable garden on one side of the yard, then darted back to their box.

"Not anymore. When I first started this hobby, I was so suited up I looked like a space alien," explained Lou. "But my bees know me now. If you handle them right, they don't bother you much. Besides, as James said, I'm used to an occasional sting."

Lou motioned for Sam to stand to one side of a hive as she slowly unlatched the hive's cotter pin and gently pulled out a tray halfway from the hive. It was covered with bees on both sides. Combs contained larvae and honey stacks. "Most of them are out foraging for pollen now, so these are the juveniles. Usually, they hatch in the spring, but we had such a hot summer that I think somebody's been busy."

Sam backed away as a few of the bees flew off the frame.

"Don't worry, dear. These are the nurse bees. They won't bother with you. Their primary charge is to take care of the hatchlings."

"How are you able to lift a full tray?"

"Oh, I have help these days. Besides, we smoke the bees out, so the tray is just honey. Then we carry the trays one at a time to the shed over there. Come on. I'll show you." Lou gently pushed the tray back into place.

"How many times do you have to empty the trays?"

"It depends on how active they've been, but generally, three times a year. Otherwise, we just let them sit. They have one more round to go, so in another few weeks, I'll strip the trays in here." Lou opened the shed door. Daylight filtered through a small window on each side. Lou flipped on an overhead light. A large stainless steel cylinder took up half of the space. Tubes from the top fed into five-gallon buckets encircling the cylinder with tops on them.

"This is where we collect the honey. It gets scraped into here." Lou struggled to lift the top. "It's like a washing machine, really. Then we spin the honey off of the combs in the tray. There are several ways to do it, but this is the most economical. Cleaning up is what takes the longest."

"What do you do with the honey?"

"Give it away, mostly. I thought it would be great to sell it to local restaurants, but I couldn't keep a consistent supply. My guests used to love it, and the sight of the hives was enough to keep them out of my backyard."

"So I wonder how a tray was out of alignment."

"Well, someone must have moved it. The cotter pin was on the ground. Unfortunately, I picked it up to put it back where it belonged, so my prints are all over it."

"Aunt Lou, your fingerprints would have been on it already from touching everything during collection time. What about your helpers? Tell me about them."

"Well, Jerry and Melvin have been with me forever. They trim the grass, tend to the gardens, paint the house.... They work for me and have for over twenty years. I wouldn't be able to run this place if they weren't helping me. And the honey collection, well, I had to talk them into it when I started doing it years ago. They still suit up. They really are a sight," Lou laughed.

"Did either have a grudge against Harvey? I mean, would either have wanted to hurt him?"

"No, they are both dears. When I learned about Harvey's daughter, I was most upset, as you can imagine. Melvin comforted me. Jerry was actually pleased, I think. If I married Harvey, Jerry was concerned that he'd be out of work. I tried to assure him that wouldn't be the case. But either way, they've been very attentive since Harvey's death, and I wouldn't suspect either of them. They are just too nice." Lou replaced the lid and walked slowly out of the shed, turning the light off behind her. "Be a dear and close that door."

Sam obeyed, then followed her back to the house, questioning her gently as they returned to the kitchen. "Did the police question Jerry and Melvin?"

"Oh, yes. They finished with both of them yesterday. They were upset, too. Back in his earlier days, Melvin had several run-ins with the law, so he was really nervous about the whole thing."

"Who else in town would know about bees?"

"I don't know. I think I'm the only person who collects them in town, but there may be someone out in the county who collects."

"Would your bees sting anyone messing with them?"

"Perhaps. You never know with bees. If they get agitated, they'll swarm."

"See, that's the problem, Aunt Lou. If your bees swarmed, couldn't they have really hurt someone?"

"Only if that person was in their path. If Harvey was outside at night and shook them up so the bees swarmed, he would have hollered. Or he'd go to the hospital. But I doubt he'd go home and go to bed."

"Would a swarm of bees stinging leave marks?"

"Oh, an attacking swarm would probably fill him with so much venom that he'd be swollen."

"Did you ever see the bees they collected from Harvey's room?"

"No, they wouldn't show them to me. I guess I'm not a reliable bee expert given the circumstances and my supposed guilt."

"I suspect if I collected the sample of bees, the police wouldn't like it, either."

"They might, if James were standing right with you."

"Well, let's see if we can make a match. I don't know the first thing about bees, but we can send a sample off to a lab to see if they match. We'll get James over here to watch me take a sample, then…."

Lou jumped to the ringing doorbell. "Speak of the devil. I'll bet that's James right now." She made her way to the door and opened it wide.

Sam cocked his head when he heard Aunt Lou exchange a polite hello with another woman.

CHAPTER THIRTEEN

"Molly!" Sam tried to act nonchalant, but his exuberance showed through.

"Hey, Dude," Molly said as she hugged Sam.

Sam remembered his manners. "Aunt Lou, this is my friend Molly Monroe from Wilmington. I asked her to come help me with my boat's engine." Sam took in Lou's look of surprise. "Really, she's a whiz with engines. Mind if I get her a cup of coffee?"

"You must have gotten an early start, dear," Lou recovered. "Come in; come in. I was just about to serve Sam another piece of blueberry coffeecake. My, you're a little thing."

Molly blushed as she followed Lou back to the kitchen. "Thank you, Lou. I would love a piece." She looked at Sam, who shrugged his shoulders. "I did get an early start. If your fuel pump is supposed to be delivered soon, I thought we'd head up to Elizabeth City to get the other pieces I'll need so we can get to work as soon as the pump gets here. Love your place, Lou. It's beautiful."

"Oh, thank you. Now, sit here." Lou motioned to the chairs at the island kitchen as she put down another plate piled high with coffeecake. "Coffee?"

"Yes, thanks." Molly smiled at Sam as she sat beside him. "Reminds me of a visit to a watering hole in Wilmington with you last spring."

"I was just thinking the same thing," Sam snickered.

"So how did you two meet?" Lou began her own line of questions. Before Molly could answer, the doorbell rang.

"Good gracious, I've had more company today than I've had in a year!" Lou walked back to the front door. Then from the foyer: "Good morning, James. You're a little late this morning," Lou said loud enough so Sam could hear who was at the door.

"Sorry, Lou. I had a staff meeting this morning. Ah, I see you have more company. If you like, I can skip today's visit."

"Don't be ridiculous, James. Come on in the house. You can meet Sam's friend Molly. She's just come from Wilmington for a visit. Besides, I made blueberry coffeecake today."

"Now you know I can't resist that." James blustered in and said hello to Molly and Sam.

"Any breaks in the case?" Sam masked his smile with his mug.

"Case?" Molly was alarmed. "Oh, no, Sam. Not again."

"It's not me, this time, Mol; it's Aunt Lou. She's been accused of something she didn't do."

"What didn't she do?"

"Honestly, do we have to do this again?" Aunt Lou smiled at the attention as she poured another round of coffee.

"Sorry," said Sam. "I'll tell her later." He turned his attention to the coffeecake.

The doorbell rang again. "Well, I declare!" Lou ambled back to the front door.

This time, it was a delivery service driver clad in brown. "Hi, Miss McClellan. I have a package here for a Sam McClellan. Can you sign for it?"

"Sure," said Lou. "Where do I sign?" she asked as the driver handed her a stylus and tablet-like device. "What in the world? Will wonders never cease?" Signing her name, Lou called to the kitchen, "Sam, where do you want this?"

"On the porch is fine." Sam next turned to Molly. "I'll be ready in a minute." He dashed up the stairs to find his shoes. He chuckled as he listened to the exchange between Molly and Aunt Lou as Molly tried to clear her plate and cup from the counter, but was shooed away by Aunt Lou.

"I'll take care of things. Just leave it there," cracked Lou. "More coffee, James?"

When Sam came back down, Molly was waiting in the large hall, a hand on the knob of the front door. He put a finger to his lips, then casually called to James. "Hey, I almost forgot, James—do you have a sample of one of the bees you guys found in Harvey's room?"

"I can get you one," came the full-mouth reply from James. "We sent several into the lab, but there are a few more there. I'll bring one around. Are you an expert on bees, now?"

"No, just curious to see what they look like. Thanks, James. I appreciate it."

"No problem. Anything for a colleague."

Sam turned to Molly and asked her whether she was ready to go.

"Dude, I'm getting a feeling I should just turn the car right around and get away from here as fast as possible." Molly was clearly uneasy, her long unkempt brown hair looking like she had just rolled out of bed.

Before they could head out of the door, Lou called, "Dinner's at six. Molly, you are welcome to stay here this evening."

"Th…thank you. I appreciate that." Molly gave Sam a quizzical look. Turning back to Lou, she added, "May the day be as bright as your smile, Lou."

"Oh, how dear. Is that some form of Irish blessing?"

Sam laughed. "No, that's just Molly. She can bless with the best of them." He omitted that she could also bestow curses on enemies like nobody's business. "Do I need to get anything for you while we're out, Aunt Lou? We're going to head to Elizabeth City for a few things a little later today."

"No," Lou called from the kitchen. "I have everything I need for dinner. See you two later."

Sam ushered Molly outside and picked up the package on the porch. His Acapulco Blue Mustang sat in the driveway, but he walked down the driveway to the sidewalk. "Come on, Molly; let's go to the boat to make sure there's nothing else we need for this job."

"I passed the marina on the way in. That's a bit of a hike."

"My boat's not in the marina. We'll need the dink to get aboard. It's on the creek just down the end of this street. Besides, I want to show you the town from the water."

"Sounds like you had a rough time. Now tell me about this case you're on."

"Technically, I'm not on it. I get the feeling these guys don't want any help." Sam told Molly all that he knew about Harvey, about his relationship with Lou, and the bees. He left out the part about his evening with Monica, though.

By the time they reached the dock in the cypress swamp, Molly was shaking her head. "Well, Dude, you can't just sit still and let her take the fall. Do you have any ideas?"

"Not yet. But I'm not leaving until I know that Aunt Lou's all right." Sam fired up the dinghy's motor as Molly hopped in and got seated. Sam steered the dinghy under the bridge, which led to the historic Albemarle Plantation land, turned high-dollar real estate development, and out into the Sound.

"You're not leaving until we get this fuel pump in," replied Molly. "Hope you have a full toolbox."

They talked about what it would take to fix the fuel pump as they boarded *Angel*. Molly took note of a few items they would need in Elizabeth City in addition to the other items Sam had ordered for this repair job. Kathy the Duck was nowhere to be seen, to Sam's relief. Sam opened all the hatches and ports in an attempt to get as much air moving through the stuffy boat as possible while they worked in the engine compartment. While it had squatting room, the engine compartment was cramped, so every bit of breeze would be appreciated, he knew.

For the rest of the morning, Sam and Molly worked on the fuel pump. They broke for lunch, motored into the marina, then walked to the West Side Deli on West Queen Street, which Molly had seen when she had to stop for gas earlier that day.

"I noticed the listing of sandwiches when I came in to pay for gas. The prices are right, and the subs look great." Molly grabbed a few bottles of water and a big bag of chips while the short man behind the counter made her an Italian sub.

Sam ordered the same, then paid for the lot. After lunch at an outside picnic table, Sam and Molly backtracked along the edge of town via the water. Once the dinghy was secure at the dock in the cypress trees, they took the Mustang to Elizabeth City to get the last needed parts and stopped by a fish market for a cooler of shrimp that Sam couldn't resist. "Aunt Lou didn't say she needed anything, but as long as we're here, we might as well be good guests."

Back on the boat, the afternoon dragged as Molly instructed Sam step by step on how to put in the new fuel pump. By five o'clock, the pump was properly installed. While they were contorted in the engine room, Sam changed the filters and the oil, too.

Sam cheered when *Angel's* engine rolled over and purred. "She's going again! Thanks, Molly."

"No problem, Dude." She looked at her watch. "We probably ought to get cleaned up. Your aunt's expecting us for dinner."

"Yeah, I know. Aunt Lou's a stickler for being on time, it seems. Hey, after dinner, would you mind ferrying me back so I can move *Angel* to the town docks? That will make it easier for me to get things done and provision again."

"I don't mind. Any excuse for a boat ride is fine with me. Now let's get going. We don't want to keep Lou waiting. Want to leave the hatches open?"

"Yeah. Nobody's going to mess with the boat way out here on the hook."

Purple and orange bathed the sky neon bright, though the humidity was slow to let go of its hold on the waning day or Sam's sweat-soaked shirt. Sam and Molly motored back to the dock in the cypress swamp. Molly got a small bag out of the Mustang's trunk, and Sam swept it out of her hand to carry it up the porch stairs.

Before he opened the front door, Sam turned to Molly, a flood of memory washing over him. "I can stay on the boat, if this is awkward," he offered. Their last night in Carolina Beach hadn't been all that he'd wanted it to be. Sam quickly replayed the night. Molly's parting words rang in his head.

"What, and leave me here alone with your killer aunt?" Molly teased. "No way, Dude."

"Seriously, if you'd prefer…."

"No, seriously, I wouldn't prefer. Besides, maybe I can help you with the case."

Reluctant to bring her into it, Sam had refused to talk about the case all day. "No. You are going back to Wilmington in the morning. I'll handle things here."

"What's the matter? Still don't want another partner?" Molly regretted the words as she watched Sam's mouth fall. "Oh, sorry, Sam. I didn't mean to bring that up again."

Sam raised his hands in the halt position. "No need to talk about it. Come on; let's go get cleaned up. I think we still have time to make ourselves presentable."

Sam carried Molly's bag up the stairs and to a bedroom opposite his. He put it on an old captain's trunk trimmed in metal at the foot of the mahogany cannonball double bed.

Molly smiled as she stepped over the threshold and took it in. "My room was this color pink when I was a little girl. Oh, look at all the little knick-knacks. And the vanity. The fabric on it reminds me of curtains I had a million years ago."

"Bathroom's down the hall. You start first. I'll go see if I can help Aunt Lou, though I already know what the answer is going to be." Sam headed back down the stairs. He didn't want to dwell on Lee's death, but there it was, staring him in the face again. Molly brought the ghosts with her, the memories, the dread Sam had tried to leave behind in Carolina Beach when he left after he sorted out who had killed his partner, his friend. Maybe it wasn't such a good idea to have her here after all.

CHAPTER FOURTEEN

As Sam entered the kitchen, he saw Lou shuffling from oven to countertop and back again, loading up serving bowls and tasting sauces. "Molly's in the shower, and I'll be cleaned up in a minute. Can I help?" He put a small cooler of shrimp on a counter, then thought better of it and placed the shrimp in the refrigerator, emptied the cooler's ice in the sink, and took the cooler outside to dry.

"If your hands are clean, you can carry these bowls to the table in the dining room. The lids will keep them warm until you get showered—which by the looks of you, you definitely need." Lou winked. "How did your work go?"

"We're done. The fuel pump is in, and the engine fired right up."

"So you're ready to go?"

"Not quite. I'm staying until we get this mess you're in sorted out."

"Well, I do appreciate your help." Lou's voice trailed off as she turned her back to Sam. "I just don't want to be a bother…."

Sam walked around the island counter and hugged his aunt. "It's not a bother."

"You *do* need a shower," Lou laughed. "Were you underwater, too?"

"No, just in the engine compartment for way too long. Perhaps you'd like to go out for a sail tomorrow. It'd be fun."

"I'd like that very much, Sammy, but I'm still under house arrest. Now get out of my kitchen and go get cleaned up, will you?"

"Wow, something smells good." Molly came down the stairs, her long brown hair still damp. "Your turn, Sam."

Sam could smell her perfume in the small kitchen. She looked great in her pale yellow cable-knit sweater and blue jeans.

"Thanks. I'll be cleaned up in a minute. And don't bother asking to help. Lou will just run you out of *her* kitchen," Sam teased.

The smell of sautéed onion and garlic pulled Sam back downstairs after a quick shower. Molly and Lou were cackling like two old hens at a story. They stopped when he entered the kitchen, then started again.

"All right, what's so funny?" Sam stood tall as Lou handed him the plates to take to the dining room.

"I was just telling Molly about the time you came to visit and you wanted to feed the ducks in the park. You chased them to the edge of the water—and fell right in." That set her off again.

"I was three, Aunt Lou."

"And you were a cute little thing."

This made Molly laugh. "Now I understand why that duck decided to adopt you in Carolina Beach."

"That duck rode with me all the way here," Sam chortled. "I can't tell you how many times I wanted to fry her up for supper."

"I didn't see her on board today."

"Thank goodness. Maybe since I've been off the boat for a few days, she's found someplace else to light."

"Speaking of supper, ours is about ready. Molly, dear, will you take this dish in, please? Sam, you take the plates."

Complying, Molly and Sam followed an empty-handed Lou to the dining room, waiting for her to adjust the crystal chandelier's dimmer switch.

"Ah, that's better. Now Sam, you sit there, and Molly, you're over here. It's so nice to have company."

"This smells fantastic," Sam said, heaping his plate with a mixture of clams, mussels, fish, and rice swimming in a rich tomato-based broth.

"It's paella, and it's one of my favorites," explained Lou. "Hope you two like seafood. Here's the bread, Molly, dear. Sam, would you please pour the wine?"

"Sure." Sam half-stood to fill their three glasses with a beautiful Shiraz.

"I don't usually drink wine, but this is so wonderful to have company, especially my favorite nephew."

"Aunt Lou, I'm your only nephew."

"I know that, but you're still my favorite." Lou winked at him. "And Molly, you've made me laugh. I'm so glad you're here, too."

"Well, thank you for your gracious hospitality, Lou." Molly beamed. "This dish is wonderful. I don't usually get a chance to cook for people, but this is one I'll definitely try."

"Maybe you could make it for Sam."

Molly blushed as she shoved a fork full into her mouth.

"I think the two of you make a cute couple," Lou continued. "Though I don't understand why Sam is sailing alone when he could have you to keep him company."

Sam butted in to help Molly. "Aunt Lou, Molly is in the process of restoring her motorboat. It's a classic, really, and it sank. She's raised it, and now she's tearing out the innards to rebuild it again."

"My, but you are talented, dear. What caused your boat to sink?"

Molly stared at Sam. "I'd rather not get into it right now, Lou. It's a long story, and, well, I'm enjoying my dinner too much to stop eating and tell you all about it. The good news is that I'll eventually have her in better shape than she was before."

Sam chimed in, "Molly delivers boats for a living, Aunt Lou, so she can't very well take time off to go for a cruise with me. Right, Molly?" Sam diverted the conversation, though he was curious about Molly's reaction to the whole thing.

"Um, right." Molly finished her wine. "How about another round?"

Sam did the honors.

"Delivering boats, fixing engines. When I was your age, dear, I didn't have the first hint at how to do any of that mechanical stuff. Even today, I have two helpers around the house."

"Well, a girl's gotta do what a girl's gotta do." Molly looked at Sam for an instant, then changed the topic. "This is excellent. Thank you for asking me to stay for supper."

"Oh, you are so welcome. Dessert, anyone?"

Sam cut Molly off before she could answer with a glance and a lean forward, suggesting he was getting up. "I think dessert will have to wait. Molly is going to help me move my boat from its anchorage to the town docks now before it gets too dark. We'll help you clear the table, though."

"No thank you, Sammy. As you know, I have a system. Now you two better scoot before it gets too dark. There'll be dessert and coffee here if you want it when you get back."

Sam and Molly said their thank yous again as they walked toward the door.

"Oh, Sam, I nearly forgot to tell you." Lou lifted her finger as if testing the wind. "The funeral is tomorrow morning at 9:30. I'd like for both of you to join me, if you don't mind."

"Of course we don't mind," Molly answered for Sam. "I didn't bring anything fancy to wear—I didn't know."

"Nothing fancy required, dear. Now have a nice night."

Walking the narrow dock through the cypress forest to the dinghy, Molly measured her words. "What did you tell your aunt about me?"

"Not much, really. She's jumped to conclusions, Mol."

"What conclusions?"

"Um, you know. That you and I are…."

"Are what?"

Sam stopped at the edge of the dock and untied the dinghy's painter. He looked at Molly, searching for a clue. Was she that oblivious, or just being coy?

"Sam?"

"She probably thinks you and I are more than just friends." Sam regretted it the moment it came out of his mouth. He'd seen the look on her face the night before he left Carolina Beach, and he'd thought she would have decked him if given the chance.

"I see." Molly got into the dinghy's stern and started the outboard. She stared off into Queen Anne's Creek, the dusky sky's reflection shattered by the small propeller.

Sam got in the bow, though that wasn't where he'd expected to sit on this ride. He pushed off the dock and pointed to the low bridge that separated the creek from the Albemarle Sound.

"Too bad I can't anchor in here," he started, "but the walk from the town docks isn't bad."

"I think I'll stay on your boat tonight so Lou doesn't get any other ideas." Molly's tone was flat.

Sam cocked his head to one side to look at her. Molly was clearly upset. What was it with her? She had pulled this same thing the last time they had seen each other. He had invited her to come sailing, but she had refused. He had suggested they could come back to Carolina Beach so she could work on her boat he had unintentionally helped to sink, but she'd gotten mad. Women. There was no pleasin' them. Sam thought it best not to say anything. Besides, it would have been hard for him to talk over the motor.

The ride through the darkening water to *Angel's* anchorage was short. Sam grabbed the hull and hoisted himself on board by stepping on the black rubber bumper that circled the boat where the hull and topside met. Holding the dinghy's painter line, Sam offered a hand to Molly, but she shook her head in refusal.

"You get her started. I'll motor back to the creek and get my stuff."

"Molly, don't do that. Look, I don't know what you expected when you came to Edenton. I'm still going sailing, you are still invited to join me, and I'll still take you back to Carolina Beach or Wilmington or wherever you want to go so you can work on your boat. I told you before I'd take you wherever you want to go whenever you want to go there. My offer still stands, and I'm being sincere." Sam held his breath.

Molly bit her lip. Then she snatched the painter line from Sam's grasp and motored back in the direction of the town dock without a word.

"What did I say?" Sam called after her, but he got no response. He fired up the engine, pleased to have some noise to drown out his thoughts.

Raising his anchor, Sam prayed for rain so he could wash the anchor and the deck off. By the looks of the sky, he wouldn't have to wait very long.

Slowly, he motored from the secure anchorage toward the town dock. Two motorboats were tucked close to shore, but the rest of the L-shaped waterfront dock was open. There was a quay separating the docks from the open Sound, so any place inside would be fine. Looking ahead, Sam could see Molly walking down the dock toward the portion closest to his approach. Sam reduced his speed to a crawl and maneuvered *Angel* inside the quay toward an open slip.

Molly walked toward that slip, still unsmiling, and waited for Sam to cast a forward line to her. She made the bow lines fast to the cleats on the dock, then got back into the dinghy and fired up the outboard.

"Molly, wait!"

"I'm just bringing the dinghy to *Angel*. You going to bring it aboard?"

"Uh, sure." Sam walked aft to wait. When Molly cut the motor off and nudged *Angel*'s hull with the dinghy's bow, Sam bent down to wait for her to toss up the painter line.

Molly handed it off to him. Then while Sam wrestled the inflatable dinghy up on the dingy davits and secured it, she climbed aboard and took a seat in the cockpit.

When he finished, Sam took a seat near Molly. "I don't have a beer to offer you. But we could get some ice cream if you want."

"Thanks; I don't want ice cream. I…I want to talk, Sam." Molly's downcast eyes were dark. "I've been thinking a lot about this. About…us."

"Us." Sam hated these talks. Whenever his ex-wife, Angel, started one of these, he always ended up sleeping on the couch.

"Yeah, Dude, you and me." Molly wasn't backing off. "We went through so much together this past summer that I thought for sure you would have been, you know, staying in town to help me with the boat, or to see what would happen with us, or…whatever. But here you are, getting into trouble again, and here I am, wondering if I should even bother."

"Bother with what?" Sam was getting the gist.

"You. You're a magnet for trouble, and I don't think I can handle any more of the results your kind of trouble brings. But the problem, Sam, is you're also a magnet for me. I can't help it. When you called the other day asking for help, I was so excited to see you again. I really had thought I'd never see you again, Sam. Now here you are, and you're still talking about sailing off into the sunset."

"Shit, Molly; I asked you to come with me. Twice! I'm just going up to Norfolk to see my son, not flying off to the moon or sailing around the world on some Don Quixote quest." Sam was getting hot. "And as for trouble, well, it's my aunt who needs the help, not me. You're not in any danger this time. Did you think I enjoyed putting you in harm's way last summer? Do you think for a second I rest easy knowing I had a hand in the loss of your boat?"

Sam's head dropped and he took a deep breath to calm down. "And anyway, I seem to recall you walking up to the whorehouse in a tight purple dress and heels. That was *you* courting trouble. That was *your* idea, not mine." He smiled at the memory.

Molly caught it and smiled, too. "You're right. That was my brilliant idea. And it worked, too."

"All I'm saying, Mol, is that I didn't drag you kicking and screaming into that hornet's nest; you dove in willingly. But I'm glad to say there's nothing going on here that is dangerous for you. Promise." Sam held his breath for a minute and looked at the sky. Clouds drifted in thick masses, darkening as they clustered. He'd get his rain tomorrow. "Mol, I…I like you. A lot. I thought of nearly nothing else on my trip up here. I thought it would be great for you to come sailing with me so we could get to know each other outside of a boiling cauldron. Then we could decide together what to do next. But you turned me down, so I kinda gave up and thought all you wanted for 'us' was to be friends." There. He'd said it.

"I had no idea, Sam," Molly whispered.

Sam caught sight of a timid little girl sitting in a woman's shapely body beside him. Never had Molly seemed so docile to him. Sam put his hand on hers on the cockpit seat and leaned in to kiss her. At the moment their lips touched, Sam could feel someone's eyes boring through his back.

"How cozy."

Reeling around, Sam froze. Monica stood just three feet away on the finger pier, her hand firmly planted on her hips.

"Oh, don't let me stop you, Sam. I'm just out for my evening walk."

"A friend of yours?" Molly's voice sounded as hard and cold as ice.

"Um, Molly, this is Monica." Sam's fear meter rose higher.

"So pleased to meet you, Molly." Monica's voice dripped. "And I do apologize for the interruption. I saw a boat come into the dock and just wanted to see if it was my racing competition for tomorrow. You remember, Sam, we're racing tomorrow evening on Paul's boat? You *are* going to come and be crew with me, aren't you?"

"The funeral is tomorrow, Monica. I'll be with Lou for the rest of the day, in case she needs me." Sam stood up in the cockpit and fidgeted with the canvas cover for the wheel. "Are you going to the funeral?"

"Oh, I don't know." Monica tossed her hair to one side and rubbed her hands seductively on her seriously tight jeans, just close enough to her crotch to make her point to Molly. Her actions reminded Sam of how his mother's cat had rubbed up against his legs when he had last visited his parents, marking Sam as his possession.

Monica walked slowly toward the boat in her stilettos, sizing up Molly. "He didn't come to Mother's, so I don't know that I need to go to his. Besides, this race is the last of the season, and it's important to win it. May I have a tour of your boat?"

"Sure." Molly stood up and jumped over the cockpit's coaming to the dock without even grabbing a stanchion. "There's plenty of room. I'm outa here." Without so much as a glance in Sam's direction, Molly walked back in the direction of Lou's house.

"Monica, now is not really a good time," Sam blurted, hoping Molly would hear. "I need to tend to my company."

"You were my company just last night, Sam. Did you forget me already?" Monica leaned over the safety lines, allowing an easy view of what was barely contained in her low-cut pale green sweater.

Sam didn't take the bait. "Look, Monica; what happened last night was, well, nothing really happened." Sam ran his finger through his short dark hair. "I didn't feel right about it, and I told you so. I had hoped that would be the end of it."

"*It* didn't happen because of Molly, right?" Monica shook her head. "Well, well. You came close to being a naughty boy. I like naughty boys. Why don't you come back to my house and let your auntie tend to your company? I think I'd like to have you for myself, and we can make *it* happen for real this time."

Ignoring Monica, Sam slid the hatch boards in place and locked the padlock. He put out two more spring lines to keep *Angel* from moving forward or backward in the slip. Then he stepped off the boat.

Monica blocked his path on the narrow finger pier. "I don't know if you didn't hear me, Sam, or if you are just trying to hurt my feelings." Monica put on a mock pout. "I had hoped all day that you would call, but now I see you've been busy with your company. What is she to you, Sam?"

Sam felt caged. "I'll see you later, Monica." He tried to sidestep her, but she moved to block him again. "Monica, I need to go. Please move."

Monica smiled eerily. "Okay, Sam. Another time?" She walked slowly backward toward the main dock, locking eyes with Sam every inch of the way.

"Yeah, Monica." Sam moved away from her and jogged off the dock after Molly.

By the time Sam reached Lou's house, the door to Molly's guestroom was already shut. Sam knocked lightly, but there was no response. Sam headed back out and sat on the wide porch. His Mustang was still in the driveway, so she hadn't bolted yet. Damn his stupidity.

Night descended quickly. Daylight savings would start next week, but already it looked like it was an hour later than it was. Sam watched treetops dance in the shadow of night, and within a few minutes, heavy rain chased him indoors and to bed. Alone.

CHAPTER FIFTEEN

Umbrellas lay tidily against foyer walls in Edenton's United Methodist Church as Sam escorted Lou into the building. They walked one step behind James Bradley, and one step ahead of Molly. Molly had been quite convincing when she told Sam earlier that morning that she'd come out of respect to Lou. She had also said she'd be leaving as soon as it was over, and her bag was in the trunk of the Mustang as proof of her intentions.

Aside from that courtesy, Sam felt Molly's anger and hurt drilling into him with each step down the green carpet that led them through a packed house of mourners.

When the foursome reached the middle of the sanctuary, James motioned Sam to help Lou into the pew.

Sam stepped out of her way, allowing Lou to move at her own pace into the pew. Then Sam nodded to James for him to sit beside her so Sam could sit beside Molly.

When Molly saw the seating arrangements, she bristled, crossed her arms, and sat. Her body language said it all.

Funerals bring out all kinds of people for different reasons. The next of kin have an obvious obligation, but town folk come of their own accord. Sam scanned the pews for Monica, expecting her, not because she was Harvey's next-of-kin as far as he knew, but because the sailing race was probably cancelled on account of the rain that had moved in overnight and was forecast to stay in the area for the day. Many of the women wore hats, so it was difficult to tell exactly who was there.

The music changed and all rose for a prayer. But before the robed minister could get started, he motioned for someone entering the sanctuary to come forward.

Sam turned his head and saw her. From her wide-brimmed black hat, the plunging neckline, all the way down to her stilettos, Monica was more appropriately dressed for a fashion runway than for her father's funeral. Clearly, she was enjoying the attention as she slowly made her way down the aisle. Beside her, looking less than thrilled to be there, was Paul in an ill-fitting suit.

Sam felt nauseous when he saw her warmly smile at him. Nausea turned to horror as Monica slowed her pace at the end of his pew as if she were going to join him.

Seeing Monica's intentions, Molly slid to the end of the pew, leaving no room for Monica and Paul.

Monica just smiled, shrugged her shoulders, then moved on to an empty pew on the sanctuary's other side.

Seeing that everyone was seated, the minister began the service for Harvey Bishop.

"We are gathered here to honor a man well-known in this community," he started. "Harvey Bishop was a good man…."

Sam tuned out the rest. He'd heard it all before, when he sat in a smaller church at the funeral of his police partner and best friend, Lee Evans. The turnout for that event was standing room only. This funeral, for a man Sam had never met, was similar in all respects. Everyone in town had come to say goodbye to a man they knew well. Everyone, Sam thought, except Molly, Monica, and himself.

When the service was over, a river of people flowed past the open casket. When the river stopped, pallbearers lifted the casket and led an umbrella-toting parade outside to a waiting hole in the adjacent cemetery. Finished with his responsibilities for the day, the minister smiled tenderly at Lou, said a few comforting words, and melted into the dismantling crowd.

Sam watched for Monica, but she was nowhere to be seen. Molly was hanging back, too, Sam noted. Perhaps she'd wait long enough for an apology or an explanation. Or both.

Then he helped Lou back to the parking lot, where James waited in a squad car. As Sam started to walk toward Molly, he brushed past a stout man hurrying toward the squad car. His umbrella aside, he held out his hand for James to stop and motioned for James to roll down the window. Sam couldn't make out all of the conversation from where he was, so he quickly weighed his options. Either he could speak with Molly now and hope for Lou to relay any conversation with this fellow, or he could double back to the squad car to listen and hope that Molly would wait. Looking back toward where Molly had stood seconds earlier, he saw no sign of her. His choice made for him, Sam jogged toward James' car. He struggled to piece together threads of the conversation when he got within hearing distance.

"Really, Lou, it's the least you could do after all Harvey and I went through together." The stout man's voice sounded agitated.

"Lester, I have absolutely no idea about that. Whatever dealings you had going on with Harvey were completely between the two of you. He made no mention of any of it to me, and I think it's atrocious for you to come around now asking about it. Poor Harvey's barely in the ground!"

Sam stood about five inches taller than the man his aunt called Lester. "Is there a problem, Aunt Lou?" He watched as Lester turned around to face him, noticing a slight hitch in his step.

"I don't think there's a problem, is there, Lester?" Lou started to roll up the window. "James, please take me home now. I've had just about enough of this kind of talk today."

James, ever accommodating, leaned over from his driver's seat and gave a small wave to Lester. "Sure thing, Lou. Sam, you want a ride?"

"No thanks, James; I've got my car here. There's something I need to do before I get back to the house."

"What about me?" Lester cried. "This conversation is *not* over yet."

"Oh, I think it's over, Mr. Crouch," James called. "At least for today. The reading of the will is in just a little while, so you'll find out if dear old Harvey thought the same way about you as you apparently did of him." With that, James rolled up the car's window and drove off, leaving Lester Crouch and Sam behind.

"What was that all about?" Sam hedged.

"Look, buster; I don't know who you are, or why James would offer you a ride back to Lou's, but that was a private conversation."

"Lou is my aunt, and I'm just here for moral support during this troubled time."

"Well, fine. You can tell your dear old auntie that Harvey owed it to me. He said as much, and I bet she knew all about it."

"Harvey owed you what?"

"The cannery! He was in debt up to his ears trying to keep it open, and I offered more than once to buy it from him. The cannery isn't worth a crap, but the land on the river there is worth a fortune. I loaned Harvey a considerable amount of money to keep the place going with the understanding that I would have first dibs on it if he couldn't pay the loans back. Since he didn't pay one red cent of his loans back, the cannery and the land is mine, fair and square."

"I assume you have that in writing?"

The look on Lester's face said it all. He puffed himself up like a rooster getting ready to fight, and spit at Sam, "We had a handshake. Around here, that's always been good enough." Lester turned on his heels and stormed off. The hitch in his step was more noticeable the faster he tried to go.

Handshake, huh? Sam was pretty sure that wouldn't hold up in a court of law even in these parts, but the reading of Harvey's will might prove interesting. Noting that his back was wet with rain, Sam worked his way across the parking lot, found his car, and headed toward Mr. Jackson's office.

One short block away, he spied Molly, working her way across a puddle in front of the office. Sam parked his car and jogged to catch up with her. "Molly, wait." He sucked in air like it was his last and ducked under her umbrella to face her. "Molly, we need to talk."

"That will have to wait. Lou asked me to come to the reading of the will for moral support, and that's exactly what I'm going to do. Then I'm leaving. Now, if you'll please excuse me…."

Sam stepped out of her way and followed her into the law office like a chastened pup. He couldn't decide whether Molly was mad or hurt—or both. Either way, he was the cause of her emotional state. He couldn't let her leave Edenton without hearing him out. It would have to keep until after the reading, though.

CHAPTER SIXTEEN

Hands neatly folded in her lap, Lou sat in a comfortable chair in front of Mr. Jackson's imposing desk. James stood beside her, more out of friendship than his appointed duty as her guard. Lester Crouch, local real estate developer, walked in and took his place near Lou, a slight bow of his head showing a balding spot on top.

Though Sam and Molly hadn't been invited to the reading, they stood firm in the back of the cramped office, the smell of old books and leather chairs surrounding them. Sam was family, after all, and Molly, well, she stood close enough to Sam so that the attorney might suspect she was related if only by marriage.

"What's he waiting for?" Sam whispered to Molly, trying to elicit any response for the day.

Molly shrugged her response. It was the most she'd done to communicate with him all morning besides asking him to get out of her way so she could come in. There was a distinct chill in the air, and not just because Sam was soaked from the morning's rain.

As if on cue, the door opened slowly. In walked Monica. Paul was decidedly absent. Monica scanned the room, her eyes settling on Sam. Then on Molly. She gracefully took her seat next to Lou, slouching casually in the wingback chair as if she were a teenager talking on a phone.

Mr. Jackson followed her into the room and took his rightful place behind his massive desk. Neatly dressed in a dark blue pinstripe suit, starched white shirt, and red tie, he wasted no time in opening the folder he carried in with him.

"Welcome, friends. Over the course of the last few months, Harvey had me change this will several times, so it took me a minute to ensure I had the most current version. I apologize for my delay. I know Harvey wouldn't have wanted this to be a formal affair, so we'll get right to the heart of it. We all know each other, I presume?" It was a rhetorical question. Not waiting for an answer, he began reading.

When Jackson got to the bequeathing, Monica bolted upright. She didn't have to wait long to hear what she clearly came for that day.

"To my daughter, Monica Maples, whose acquaintance I've just recently made, I leave my collection of books. They have provided me much enjoyment over the years, and I hope she will enjoy them as well. To my dear old friend

Lester Crouch, I leave my fleet of boats in various conditions to repay his debt of kindness to me. And to my longtime confidant, friend, and the person I have for decades considered to be my significant other, Lou McClellan, I leave the rest of my estate to enjoy in whatever fashion she desires for as long as she shall live." He paused.

"He said he would include me," Monica snarled.

"I believe he did, my dear," Jackson replied. "Your father had an extensive collection of some of the finest books I've ever seen. Now, shall we continue?" Jackson looked to the rest of his audience.

With a nod from them, he finished his duties with the will. When pressed, Jackson gave a copy of the will to Sam so he could review it. Lou's inheritance included Harvey's house, the cannery and its surrounding property, plus a sum of close to three million dollars.

Sam watched his aunt for a reaction.

Lou cried softly, her head bent. She didn't seem surprised at her increased fortunes, just sad.

Lester was incensed. "Harvey Bishop owes me much more than those crappy boats of his! He promised me the land on which the cannery sits in exchange for all the money I've loaned him over the years! He was in debt up to his eyeballs. How can he leave you that kind of money? It's all mine!"

"Now, now, Les, we are all saddened by Harvey's passing," soothed Jackson. "I know nothing of other debt owned. If it wasn't on paper, legally, it didn't exist. So if you care to contest, we'll save that for another day."

"You mean there could be a redistribution of assets in the future?" Monica was keen to learn the answer.

"Could *have* been, my dear." The lawyer shuffled the papers in front of him. "If Mr. Bishop passed away *after* Lou, this conversation certainly would have been different." He cleared his throat before proceeding. "In the event of Lou's death, Harvey directed me to split his assets between a few of his close friends, including Lester. A small sum of money would have come to you in that event, Monica."

"But he had to die first. Great." Monica was on the edge of her seat.

"Everything goes to Lou," Jackson answered flatly.

"I'm going to contest this," said Lester, still fuming.

"That's fine, Lester. Have your lawyer contact me tomorrow and we'll start the process. There's no guarantee how long it will take, though. Right now, I am sure Lou is ready to rest a bit. Thank you all for coming." Jackson stood and straightened his tie, signaling to the others that the event was over.

Single file out the door, the small group walked to their cars. Monica paused and eyed Lou, then approached her slowly, cautiously, like a cat stalking a bird.

"I am sorry for your loss, Miss McClellan, and frankly, surprised by your gain. My beloved father must have thought a great deal of you."

"We were going to be married." Lou didn't bother to turn around to face Monica. She focused on getting into the car as James assisted her by holding her arm.

James piped up. "When you are ready to collect your books, I'll send someone to help you, Miss Maples. It's going to be a truckload."

"Thank you, Officer Bradley. I'll keep that in mind." Monica stood still for a moment, her back ramrod straight, apparently not the least bit bothered about the rain now drenching her clothes. Turning to Sam, she cooed, "Sam, it was so nice of you to come to the service today for my father. I had hoped you would stop by for…tea, but I see your company is still here." Monica nodded ever so slightly toward Molly, who stood two steps away from Lou: close enough to hear and see the meaning Monica intended to send. Monica took a step closer to Sam, then thought better of it, and headed to her car, not making an effort to open her umbrella.

CHAPTER SEVENTEEN

"Hop in; I'll give you a ride back," James called to Molly, who was halfway to Oak Street.

"No thanks; I need the exercise. I'll see you there in a minute."

Sam slowed his car, parked it quickly three feet behind Molly, and got out to walk with her. "Molly, we need to talk," he started.

"Sam, there's no need. I made a fool of myself last night on your boat. I'm really angry at myself, not you."

"Molly, you have every right to be mad at me. I…well, I had no idea you were interested in me that way. And Monica threw herself at me, and, well, I was…."

"You were tempted. What man wouldn't be? She's seriously gorgeous—in fact, she's seriously hot, and well, I'm not all that, anyway. Really, it's not a problem, Dude."

"Look; nothing happened, despite what she wants you to think. You have to believe me. I wasn't tempted or anything."

Molly kept on marching, her eyes still straight ahead. "You don't have to explain anything to me, Sam. You and I aren't an item, so you didn't do anything wrong."

"We could be."

"We could be what?" Molly stopped at the corner of Oak and Queen Streets to face him.

"We could be an item." Sam pulled her close. "We were interrupted last night. I want to finish what we started." He planted his lips on hers, holding her tightly.

Molly didn't resist.

As Sam opened his eyes, he saw Lou watching them from her front porch two houses away. She was smiling.

"I think we're expected." Sam turned Molly around so she could see Lou waving them in like a nervous mother waving her kids in from their fun spot too far out in the ocean.

"I should be getting back, anyway." Molly stepped in the direction of Lou's as the rain poured down. "I'm cold."

"Me too. I'll go get my car and meet you back here in a minute. I'm sure Lou's got some coffee going."

As he pulled into the driveway, Sam saw Molly still outside. He jogged to the porch and took the steps two at a time to stand beside her. As they came in the door, Lou greeted them with towels and instructions to take off their wet things upstairs.

"Soup will be ready in just about thirty minutes. Get into some dry clothes, you two. James, you'll stay for lunch, I hope?"

"I never pass up your cooking, Lou. Come on; I'll help you get it ready."

"No, James; you'll just sit where I tell you to. It's my kitchen...."

Sam smiled as he headed up the stairs after Molly. "You want a shower?"

"Are you joining me?" Molly whispered.

Sam thought about it for a second or two. "We probably oughta wait." He couldn't believe what came out of his mouth.

"That's fine. I was only kidding, Sam." Molly smiled as she closed the door to her room.

Sam sighed heavily as he took off his rain-drenched khakis and blue button-down shirt. He toweled off, assessed his lean body in the mirror, and then searched the closet for something clean to wear. Time to do laundry.

A faint tap at his door made him jump. Still naked, he opened it slowly, then wider as he saw Molly. Her long wet hair dripped rivulets down her naked breasts.

"Is this waiting long enough?" she whispered. She tiptoed into Sam's room and dove for the unmade bed.

"You sure about this?"

"Yep."

Sam closed the door in hopes of stifling whatever noises he and Molly were about to make.

When they were finished, Molly got up and tiptoed to the bathroom. Sam could hear the shower running. He toweled off, dressed, and walked downstairs. He couldn't wipe the silly grin off his face.

James caught sight of him first. He grinned, too. Apparently, James had better hearing than Lou.

By the time Molly joined them, Sam, Lou, and James were sitting at the dining room table. Sam was pouring sherry for Lou, and a wine bottle sat on the table in front of the empty space. James was sipping on his beer.

"Excellent, as always, Lou." James pointed to his soup presented in a blue and white china bowl. "I never quite understood why you didn't open a restaurant."

"I thought about it once, but the bed and breakfast seemed to be enough work for me. Besides, Edenton already has enough fine restaurants. I wasn't even able to supply them all with enough honey."

"Oh! That reminds me." James put down his soup spoon and pulled a small clear plastic bag from his trouser pocket. "I nearly forgot about it, but here's a sample of the bees we found in Harvey's room." James tossed it lightly across the table to Sam. "We sent one just like it to the National Wildlife people, but haven't heard back from them yet."

"It's not much to look at." Sam handed it to Lou. "Can you tell if this is one of yours?"

"I can tell you it's not." Lou sat up straight. "I use Starline bees. They are a hybrid of Italian bees. You might know them as clover bees. But they are excellent producers and have a very docile temperament."

"How can you tell this isn't one of yours?" Sam asked.

"Because of the swarming activity," Molly chimed in. "It takes an awful lot to make Starlines swarm. This is probably an Africanized honey bee. Were there many found in the room?"

Sam stared at Molly. "And how do you know so much about bees?"

"Yep," interjected James. "At least two dozen."

"It's most likely an Africanized honey bee, then. My dad used to keep bees, and we had problems in the hive one summer after a very mild winter. See, when you have a healthy hive, you can get a swarm. If the colony is healthy and large, a scout will leave the hive and go out in search of a new place. Over half of the bees in a solid hive will leave with the old queen once a new queen comes along. They will fly together, and often land nearby, waiting on the scout to come back with news of their next home. The African bees are aggressive, and if they get into the mix, the swarm can become a mess. I remember that the Agricultural Extension Service representative came out to our place to collect the swarm. We all had to take a beekeeping course when we were kids before Dad started *that* adventure. The only way to tell for sure is to send it off to a lab."

"I agree, Molly," said Lou. "James, why didn't you bring this to me before?"

"Well, Lou, I had no idea it was any different than what you keep out back. Besides, you can't be an expert witness in your own case." James stuffed his mouth full of French bread. "I'm sure the wildlife or lab people will come up with the same answer. Then you'll be off the hook."

"Have you ever had a swarm of Africans in your hive, Lou?" Molly quizzed.

"Not that I know of. There have been a few spotted south of here, in Beaufort, but none in Edenton. I thought it was too far north for them."

"Not necessarily," Molly explained. "They are tropical bees, but I think they are adapting. They came into Morehead City on a cargo ship in the 1990s. Ever since then, they are spreading. The only problem is they can't hold a lot of food, so they usually die over the winter."

"So a stray swarm of African bees did it?" Sam piped up. "Sounds like something out of a bad movie."

"Maybe," answered James. "But how did they get into Harvey's bedroom? And wouldn't he have swatted them down or something?"

"Africanized bees can fly pretty fast, and they don't give up easily," offered Molly. "They're extremely aggressive, and their stings can be deadly, especially to the elderly or to those with poor immune systems."

"Well, Harvey was in great shape for a man his age." Lou smoothed back her hair. "And we don't like to be referred to as 'elderly,' my dear."

"I'm sure she didn't mean anything by it, Aunt Lou," Sam interceded. "Anyway, how would the swarm get in? James, may I have permission to enter the crime scene?"

"Sure. I'll have to go back to the station to get a key."

"Or you could use mine," offered Lou.

A knock at the door interrupted their conversation. Sam excused himself to open the door, but he called Lou when he found himself peering at about twenty upturned faces standing in a line that spilled off the porch and down the street toward the waterfront. Many huddled under umbrellas too small for the gang they were meant to protect.

"We come to pay our respects," said a rail-thin black man in a shiny black coat and dress slacks. He carried a felt fedora as creased as his face in his right hand, and a small box wrapped in red paper in his left. He waited patiently as Lou ambled to the door and opened it wide.

"Miss Lou, me and everybody just want to let you know we are real sad about Mister Harvey," he started when he saw Lou step into the doorway.

Sam moved back behind her, bumping into Molly and James.

"Hello, Gus. Thank you for coming," whispered Lou. "Good gracious, you've brought a lot of people with you!"

"Yes'm," Gus replied, a tickle of a smile playing at the corner of his dark mouth.

"Won't you all please come in?" Lou stood aside in hopes of having them all come in out of the rain. "We have plenty of lunch available for everyone."

Gus shook his head and held his position on the porch. "No, ma'am, we just come to pay our respects. We all owe Mister Harvey in one way or another, and we mean to pay it back somehow." Gus gave Lou his box, bowed, and stood off to the side to watch the next person in line advance. "You may not recognize all these folks. We have each worked for the fish house at one point, and we each got help when we needed it most. And you know who stepped in to help? Mister Harvey, that's who. For me, he personally drove me to the electric company and paid my bills one cold winter when my wife got laid off from her job in town. For Eddie and Mae here," Gus pointed a finger at a solemn man who assisted his elderly wife up the last step to the porch, "he brought a carload of groceries when Mae was having their fifth child."

Eddie tottered to Lou and placed a thin brown manila envelope in her hands. "These are pictures of our children he's provided for all these years. Me and Mae both work…worked for him, and a better boss we never had."

Mae's eyes welled up. "He's going to be missed." She blew her nose in a small hankie, then took Eddie's outstretched arm and sat down in the hanging porch swing. Eddie took a seat beside her, and they rocked gently back and forth, setting a cadence for the line as it swelled on the porch like a gentle ocean wave at the shore.

Gus explained everyone's story of how Harvey Bishop had helped them through troubled times as each person presented his or her offering to Lou. Harvey had paid a lot of overdue bills, delivered carloads of groceries, paid better than any other employer out in the county, drove people to doctors' visits, and even helped a couple on the brink of foreclosure by buying their home and then gifting it back to them.

Everyone whom Harvey had helped over the years added details to Gus' version of the story before offering a small, meaningful token to Lou. Lou handed each gift respectfully back to James, Molly, or to Sam, who laid the gifts on the dining room table.

"We don't know what you're planning to do with the cannery, but we are hopeful you will keep it open. We all promise to work real hard for you, too. There ain't no other jobs up there, and we would rather work for reduced wages to pay back our debt than to clean a toilet for some of the new people coming to town." Gus motioned with his arm the way one might swish a toilet bowl with a brush. "You don't have to answer now, ma'am; we just want to state our case. See, Mister Harvey was a good man." Gus stated matter-of-factly. "He gave us work when he really had none to give, and we all know that. And he paid for work that we sometimes couldn't do because we was sick or injured." A slight murmur of agreement ran through the crowd on the porch. "Mister Harvey, ma'am, well, he was a saint!" Gus yelled.

A chorus of "Amen!" rang out, followed by a low but audible rumble of an old gospel song that picked up volume as it rolled along. The verses continued as Gus shook Lou's hand and stepped off the porch. Gus' cohorts followed suit, each shaking Lou's frail hand or hugging her and then walking back to the sidewalk, again huddling under umbrellas. When the porch was clear, Gus held up his hands like a concert hall conductor. The singing stopped. Dramatically, Gus looked at his choir lining the sidewalk or standing in damp grass. Then with vigor, he swooped his arms up and down like a stunted bird preparing for flight. On the exact same beat to imaginary music, the group started singing again, only this time it was a rousing version of a song about saints going marching into heaven.

Slowly, the group disbanded and got into a variety of cars—old and new, fast and slow. With lights on for respect, the procession moved up the road as the rain stopped. Soon, the sun peeked out from behind a mask of clouds as if Harvey's former employees' message had been heard.

Molly and Sam carried the last of the gifts to the dining room and spread them out for Lou to inspect. For the first time, Lou didn't seem to notice Molly clearing the table or running the water to rinse the plates and glasses in her kitchen.

James watched as the last of the visitors drove away, and then he shut the door before joining Lou and her treasures.

Lou opened each gift slowly, admired it, and put it aside. If there were a tag or a note on the gift, she carefully read it, then jotted a note on a piece of paper.

"What's the list for?" James wiped his eyes with a napkin.

"I want to thank these people. They didn't have to do this. And I am sure that these gifts are their treasures. They didn't have to do this," she repeated.

Tattered black and white photos of loved ones, small shots of men wearing fedoras standing in front of the cannery or behind a counter with aprons on, and pictures of men in boats struggling to pull nets loaded with shining fish were frequent. A total of eighty-six dollars and twenty-five cents crammed a small peanut butter jar. A collection of comic books with a red ribbon neatly tied around them, a carved bird whistle, handmade fishing lures crafted from bits of different species of wood and assorted boa feathers, a three-inch high sailboat made of toothpicks, a handful of Indian arrowheads, a cut-glass candy dish, a necklace of tarnished silver with a small fish charm, a box of chocolates, a bottle of rum, and another envelope, this one a thick white one, stuffed with bills totaling three hundred and seventy-four dollars rounded out the loot, all gifts of respect for Harvey Bishop.

Lou put her head down on her arms and sobbed. "They can't know how much this means to me. Harvey was always kind, but I didn't know he was this *good.*"

James comforted her with gentle pats on the back. "There, there, Lou. It's an emotional time. You want me to box this stuff up?"

"No, James," Lou said as she sat up straight. "Let's put it to good use. Sammy, I'm going to need your help."

"You've got it," Sam answered. He grabbed for Molly's hand. "We're ready to do whatever you need done."

CHAPTER EIGHTEEN

Sam and Molly drew sketches and took measurements of the gifts Gus and his friends had given to Lou, discussing the merits of glass or its substitutes for a display case while James finished off his third cup of coffee.

"It's going to take me about forty-five minutes to drive up to Elizabeth City," James stood up, stretching his arms overhead. "The hardware store here isn't going to have it all. I'll be back in about three hours or so."

"Sounds good," Sam answered. "Aunt Lou, we're going to get my tools off *Angel.* Will you be all right by yourself for a bit?"

Lou laughed and started to push her chair back from the table. "I could use some alone-time. I think I need a nap. Three hours' worth will be just right for me to take a bath and a nap. Just let yourselves in when you get back."

Sam gave James a list of needed supplies. "We should have this list knocked out in about an hour or so, or at least by the time you get back."

James nodded, pulling at his tie. "I'm going to swing by my house to change. Do you have all the tools you need, or shall I bring back some of mine?"

"I think we've got all we'll need," Sam called over his shoulder. He took the stairs by twos, grabbed his wallet and sandals, and was back down before James had left. "You look puzzled, James. What's up?"

James opened his door and looked in the driveway. "Don't think it's all going to fit in my car," James muttered more to himself than to Sam. "I'll have to get the truck instead." He ambled outside. "Looks like the rain stopped. We can work in the backyard." Then he stepped off the porch, heading for his car.

"Three hours or so," Molly whispered over Sam's shoulders.

Sam turned to see her Cheshire cat grin. He stepped aside to let her step out the door first. "You want to drive?"

Molly nodded and drove along the waterfront. The city's town docks were no busier than they had been the day Sam sailed into Edenton Bay. "Too bad we don't have time for a sail. It's been a while since I was at *Angel's* helm."

"Yeah, three hours isn't much time for a decent sail. We'll just have time to look at the charts and gather the tools we need." Sam pulled *Angel* closer to the dock for Molly to step aboard.

"Thanks. Now where are your tools?" She was beaming.

Sam climbed aboard, taking in the town's view. He spied Monica slowly walking across the park's diagonal sidewalk, heading right toward the docks.

"We're heading out." He unlocked the hatches, grabbed the key, and fired up the engine before Molly could say anything. "You take the helm. I'll throw the lines."

Quickly, Sam untied spring lines, bowlines, and pulled on the aft lines before Molly had the boat in reverse. "Give her some juice, Mol. I'll fend her off."

Molly did as she was instructed. *Angel* responded, her full keel sluggish in reverse. It wasn't until she had the boat completely turned around and heading out that she saw Monica, hands on hips, frozen in front of the park swings.

"Oh. Evasive tactics?"

Sam didn't say a word as he dove below and grabbed the chart book. "Albemarle Sound has good water and lots of creeks, but one in particular looked interesting. Bachelor's Bay looks nice. We'll have to cross the Chowan River to get to it."

"I thought we didn't have enough time."

"We have time for a sail over and back, just to catch some air. Then I think we'll anchor out and take the dink back to that creek near the condos. It won't take long to get the tools together. You want some water? I think that's about all I've got."

"That's hardly good provisioning, in case you have to escape Edenton." Molly sat down and steered with her foot.

"Yeah. I'll have to work on that."

"Is there any interest at all?"

Sam looked up from his chart. "In Monica? Not a bit." He scooted toward Molly's seat and put his hand on hers, leaning over to kiss her.

Molly returned his affection, then turned her attention back to the approaching channel markers. "Which way to Bachelor's Bay? Sounds like a great place to be."

Osprey flew from cedar to pine along the tree-lined shore as Sam and Molly slowly passed. A slight breeze pushed *Angel* along until they reached the entrance to the Chowan River. There, the wind whipped up froth, and *Angel* heeled as Sam pulled in the main and jib.

"Woo-hoo!" Molly yelled. "I haven't seen this kind of wind since…I don't remember when!"

Sam backed off the sheets a little. "She rides well with the wind, not so well in light stuff. There. Hold her right there."

The reach was great until the other side of the Chowan River, where trees blocked the wind sufficiently to set *Angel* down squat in the water. The tree line broke, and a tight cove appeared.

"Bachelor's Bay," Sam pointed. "We've got plenty of room…just not enough time to drop the hook."

"No problem," said Molly. "It's a great place. Maybe we can come another time. You ready to take her back?"

"I guess." Sam stood up to take the helm. "Up there is the Salmon River, though I can't imagine salmon here in fresh water."

Molly looked at the chart. "You better be wondering if there's a safe anchorage closer to the condo creek." She sounded worried. "It's open, see? If we get a strong blow, *Angel's* likely to feel it."

"Then we'll put her back in the anchorage where I had her before. I just don't think I want her at the town dock anymore."

Molly grinned. "Afraid, are we?"

"Cautious." Sam looked toward the Chowan River's entrance and adjusted the sheets. "No need to put the boat in harm's way."

"Monica seems pretty harmless now that we've got things sorted out."

"Yeah, I guess." Sam wasn't convinced. "She's just not… well, she's taking this like she's been dumped, first by me and now by her dear old dad. I think it's best just to stay out of her way."

"Speaking of her dad, we probably should go see the house."

"I did that already, the night I got here. It looked like a topsy-turvy version of Aunt Lou's."

"Harvey wasn't a neat-freak?"

"Well, let's just say he didn't have 'systems' the way Aunt Lou does. His place is filled with books, old furniture, and his cupboards were bare."

"Because he gave all his food away," Molly finished his thought. "But what about him? What about the bees?"

"It was too dark to see anything when I was in there. We'll take a look after we finish the display cabinet."

"That's a nice thing for Lou to do." Molly braced herself for the wind whipping down the river. "Do you think the chamber will accept it?"

"Yeah, I get that Harvey was beloved by the town, and this might be the thing to clear Lou's reputation."

"What about her guilt? That's what we need to clear." Molly slid toward Sam's seat. Her movements didn't go unnoticed.

"Uh, we'll find out what happened. Here comes the river. It's going to get bumpy in that wind. You ready?"

"Yep. Bring it on."

A mix of wind and spray whipped her long dark hair into her face. She reached to pull it back with one hand while holding on to the boat's coaming with the other. To Sam's way of thinking, Molly was far more tempting than Monica would ever be.

By the time *Angel* reached the calmer waters on the other side of the river, Sam's finger had traced the Chowan's outline on the chart up to the point where the cannery was. Quick calculations of distance and speed told him what he needed to know. The cannery land could be a perfect community if developed by someone like Lester Crouch. Sam smiled at the thought of a gated place, a guard assessing the worthiness of potential visitors as they approached a main entrance surrounded by expensive bricks with exotic species of palm trees.

"What's so funny?" Molly asked.

"I'm just imagining the kind of swank neighborhood someone like Lester might want to develop on the cannery land, complete with tennis courts and posh homes and picket fences to make it look all 'village-y.' How absurd dear old Harvey Bishop would think it all was. From what I gathered, he didn't seem much like the country club set."

"Yes, I can see it now," Molly played along. "Bishop's Landing." She giggled. "Have you been to the cannery?"

"I have—it was a bit of a mess, though. It's hard to imagine it hanging on for much longer, given its current condition. I'll run you up there tomorrow so you can see it for yourself."

"Oh, Sam, you always take me to the best places." Molly fluttered her eyelashes and smiled. She leaned in to kiss Sam just as *Angel* made her way past the town dock. Molly scanned the park. "Looks like the coast is clear. Mind if I take her in while you get ready to drop the hook?"

"That's fine." Sam climbed forward to the bow, keeping an eye on the cypress trees lining the fairway. Scanning the water closest to the park, he noticed someone on the balcony of the landlocked lighthouse. It only took a second to figure out who it was: Monica walked slowly along the length of the balcony, matching *Angel's* progression past the protected docking area. Sam had a clear view of her and watched her lean on the railing. Even from this distance, he could tell she was glaring at him.

CHAPTER NINETEEN

Sam lowered the hook in the cove and dropped the dinghy from its davits while Molly secured the hatch boards. Sam rowed them to the town docks, and Molly climbed up on a narrow finger pier so she could bring his car back to Lou's house.

"I'll meet you down by the condo dock," Sam called as he rowed, cursing himself for not remounting the small outboard.

He slipped out from the protected waters of the pier and hugged the shoreline toward Queen Anne's Creek, ducking under the bridge that led to the former plantation land-turned-swank community of Albemarle Plantation. Soon, he reached the shallow waters near the condo building, his back drenched from rowing.

Molly helped unload the tools from the dinghy and put them in the trunk of the Mustang. "Think we have enough?"

"We have what we need," Sam said, climbing into the passenger side door. "You drive." It was a quick drive to the house.

"You're late," James scolded, a paper cup of coffee in one hand and their set of plans sprawled out on the front porch beside him. James dangled his feet off the side like a kid fishing on a dock. "Lou's still resting, but I know she'll be out here as soon as we get started. You get what you needed?"

"I got what I have," Sam replied, shrugging his shoulders and lifting a circular saw, orbiting sander, and a tool bag filled with assorted sandpaper, screwdrivers, and screws out of the trunk.

Molly stepped out of the car and walked around to the trunk. She helped lug the tools toward Lou's backyard where James had neatly stacked several sheets of plywood, lumber, and trim pieces. Five small sheets of glass leaned against the honey shed, one for each side and top of the case.

"Think we'll wake up the bees?" James looked nervously at the beehive.

"They're probably out foraging," Molly assured him. She walked by the length of the fence separating Lou's yard from Harvey's, noting the dip in it. "While you two he-men get started, I think I'll have a look-see next door."

"I'll go with you, Mol," Sam called. "We'll only be a minute, James."

"Sure, just leave me here with the work," James chided. "You got Lou's key?"

Sam patted his pocket. "Yep. We won't be long."

Approaching the back screened door of Harvey's house, Sam looked at the window to Harvey's bedroom. "Look at this."

Molly caught his stare. Her hands confirmed his thoughts. "Stapled. From the outside. Either Harvey didn't know how to repair a blown screen or we got us a clue. Let's go see what else we can find."

Entering the back door, Molly and Sam passed the washing machine and dryer. Lou's key opened the interior door. A musty smell greeted them as they entered.

"Phew. I'll bet ol' Monica's going to be happy cleaning those out." Molly held her nose. "Harvey wasn't much on cleaning, was he?"

"Come on. Look in here." Sam opened cupboards in rapid succession. "There's not much in here. Guess he gave it all away."

"Do you think he knew?"

"He changed his will several times, according to Mr. Jackson. Maybe he had a suspicion his time was near."

"But why? He was clearly loved by everyone in town."

"Not necessarily. I can think of two people who didn't feel that way. Maybe there are more." Sam reviewed the ceiling-high shelves of books. "Wonder if he actually read all of them."

Molly didn't wait to take inventory. "His bedroom is... here." She turned the corner and was greeted by the police tape. She looked under the bed first. "More bee carcasses. When did you say he died?"

"A few days before you got here. Why?"

"These bee bodies are way older than that. See how some don't even have their heads or legs anymore? That's a later stage of decay. These bees have been here longer than just a few days."

"Or they're a plant." Sam stood up and looked around the room. "Did you notice the books?"

"Yeah, they're everywhere. Hope Monica's got a big house."

"She doesn't. But that's not what I'm talking about. Look at that stack. Don't you see? Everywhere in this house are messy piles and piles of books. Here's a stack of thick books under the window, like some sort of ladder."

"Someone's been in—or out through that window," Molly agreed. "Wonder if Harvey kept his windows locked."

"Not this one," Sam noted. "I checked the last time I was here. It was dark, so I couldn't see well."

"What's his last choice in literature?" Molly was on her hands and knees by the bed, studying book titles. "A few contemporary murder mysteries, *The Beginner's Guide to Marine Biology*, and some fishing guides. Nothing unusual."

"Seen enough?" Sam stood to leave. "I'm sure James is ready to get started."

"Sure, Dude. I'm ready to get some splinters."

James scowled when Molly and Sam climbed back over the fence into Lou's backyard. "Took you long enough."

"Sorry, James," Sam said. "We just wanted to see everything in the daylight."

"I suppose that would be easier than touring at night, even on a night when the moon is full." James leaned back, putting his hands on his expanded girth.

Sam snorted and shook his head when he realized he'd been seen touring Harvey's house the first time. He changed the subject and picked up a turned wooden leg. "Um, I like the legs you chose for this case."

"They don't go on yet," James smiled. "Here. Hold that end of this plywood while I cut." James waited for Sam to get to the other end of the sawhorse. "Steady." James cut the sheet with the circular saw, then moved to the other end and cut again, following pencil lines he'd made on the board.

The three focused on their project for the rest of the afternoon, leery of the occasional bee flying by inspecting the sources of the noise.

Lou called out the back door at suppertime. "Food's on the table, crew. Come and get it. Oh, this is so much fun! I have guests again!"

Molly was the first to put down her sandpaper. "Great! I'm starving. Come on, fellas; don't be rude."

Sam and James followed. After washing hands, the three sat down at the dining room table while Lou poured water in their glasses like a fussy waitress.

"You've got sawdust all over you, Sammy. And James, you've torn your shirt. I hope you've not been overdoing it."

"Lou, I'm fine. This old shirt's my work shirt. It's got more rips in it than I've got years on me!"

"Well, just the same, I appreciate all you are doing for me. Now dig in."

No more encouragement was needed. Sweet potatoes, fried chicken, fresh peaches drizzled with honey, green beans, and homemade dinner rolls beaconed. Conversation quickly gave way to forks and knives working.

After supper, Lou inspected the project. "It's perfect. I can't thank you enough for making this. I've called Sal Edwards at the Chamber of Commerce. She said she'd be delighted to have it, and that she'll be at the chamber building tomorrow to help upload it if someone can bring it by."

"No problem, Lou; I'll be by first thing in the morning and take it in on my way to work. Sam can help me load it in the truck."

"Wonderful, James. I would appreciate that. When you're finished with it, just move it into the honey shed. Oh, thank you for doing this!"

James hugged her gingerly. "Lou, it's a grand thing that you're doing. I'm only sad we had to lose Harvey to see how much everyone loved him. Now let's get you back inside before you get chilled. These two can finish up and put away all the tools, right, Sam?"

"Right, James. We won't be long. Just have to put the glass in." Sam turned his attention to the project, and Molly joined him in finishing the case. "With a piece of cloth in the bottom, it'll show off those things everyone brought nicely."

"Yeah." Molly lifted a small piece of glass and fitted it to the back. "All for a favorite son."

CHAPTER TWENTY

Sam woke to the whine of fishing boat motors racing on the Sound. Their high pitches waned and then stopped as the fishermen reached their favorite spots. Sam imagined what it would be like to work on the water all day for a bucket of fish. He came to the conclusion that when he finally got the motor fixed and his boat ready to go cruising for a while, he would find out, but at a more leisurely pace. Reaching out for Molly, he felt an empty spot where she'd been the night before.

Sweet cinnamon rose up the stairwell, pulling Sam out of bed and down the stairs. He saw Molly on a kitchen stool, cup of coffee in hand, flipping the pages of a newspaper.

"Morning, Sam," Molly called out.

"Morning, Molly, Aunt Lou. You're up early."

"Oh, nothing new for either of us, dear," Lou spoke first. "Molly was out on the front porch when I stepped out to get the paper."

"I didn't have a key to get back in. I enjoyed the breeze on the porch."

"What were you doing up so early?" Sam took the stool beside her, nodding to Lou as she placed a mug of coffee in front of him.

"I went for a run. Edenton is a great town for running. All the streets are wide and flat, and there's lots to look at down by the waterfront."

"Breakfast will be ready in just a minute, Sammy." Lou was pulling something out of the oven, hiding it from her audience, as it were.

"See anything of interest on your run?" Sam quizzed.

"A few boats out. That was it. Just a quiet run around town." Molly sipped her coffee. "What are you making, Lou?"

"A cinnamon-glazed coffeecake filled with raspberries. Harvey picked them near his cannery last summer. There were so many that I froze several bags. We've enjoyed them quite a bit." Lou frowned at the thought of Harvey, then shrugged and cut into the coffeecake. "It's ready, if you two are."

"Absolutely!" Molly was up offering assistance, but she was promptly shooed away.

"So what's on the agenda for today, Sam?" Molly asked as she tucked into the coffeecake.

"Thought we might run up the road to see the cannery while we're waiting for results on the bee bodies from the lab. Is there anything we can get for you while we're out, Lou?"

"Not a thing," Lou answered as she served another piece to Sam. "If you like, I'll make you a picnic lunch. Will you be sailing or driving?"

"Driving this time. It's looking like it might rain," Sam said as he craned his neck to see dark clouds filling the window's view. "A picnic might still be nice, though. Thanks, Aunt Lou."

Lou seemed distracted. "Aunt Lou, is something the matter?"

"James isn't here, yet. I hope he's not taken ill."

"He's probably just running a little late. He's supposed to help me load the cabinet into the truck and take the tokens today to the chamber. Maybe he wanted to clean out the back of the truck or get a tarp to keep the rain off."

"It's not like him, though. He's been coming here each morning like clockwork. Sammy, would you please call the police station just to be sure he's okay? I've got the number written near the phone."

"Sure," Sam said as he got up and moved toward the phone. "I'm sure he's...." Sam was interrupted by a knock at the door. "See? He was just running a little late today."

Sam changed course toward the foyer and opened the door for James. "Not to worry, Aunt Lou; he's here. And just in time—I was thinking about having another piece of coffeecake." James didn't move from the doorway. "James? What's wrong?"

"Can we talk? Outside?" James' tone was hushed.

"We'll be right in, Aunt Lou," Sam called as he shut the door behind him and gestured toward the porch chairs. "What's the matter, James? Something's happened?"

"There's been a break-in this morning. I was called to investigate."

"Two crimes in one month? What's Edenton coming to?"

"Sam, it was Monica Maples' house."

"Was she hurt? Was anything taken?"

"No, Ms. Maples had already left for the morning. She came back home because she said she'd forgotten to feed her fish, and she noticed the back door was unlocked. When she went in, she said she noticed things seemed out of place. None of her valuables were missing, though."

"Did she indicate what was out of place?"

"A high school yearbook was open on her coffee table the night before. She said she'd been reminiscing about old friends. I guess the loss of her father has made her feel nostalgic or something. Anyway, she said the book was not turned to the correct page."

"Okay, so maybe a breeze blew a page. And in a town like this, I bet lots of people leave their doors unlocked."

"There's more, Sam."

"I'm listening."

"An old letter was missing. She said it was tucked in the yearbook, toward the back."

"From?"

"A letter from Harvey. To Monica's mother. The boys did a quick check and found she died a few years back."

"Any idea what the cause was?"

"Obit didn't say much, but after a few calls, they came up with a heart attack."

"Curious."

"How so?"

Sam bluffed to gain some time. "Just curious that Monica would carry such a letter in a yearbook." Recounting his conversations with Monica earlier, he wondered what really happened. "Any leads on who might have broken in?"

"More of an unhappy coincidence. As I turned into Ms. Maples' driveway, I saw someone climbing over the back fence."

"Sounds like a suspect. Why unhappy?"

"It sure looked a lot like your girlfriend, Molly."

CHAPTER TWENTY-ONE

A wary look on his face, James walked into the kitchen, followed by Sam. Molly and Lou were looking at a roadmap of the area. Lou was being the nostalgic tour guide.

"Up in this area is where we used to find loads of arrowheads. You and Sammy might want to have your picnic there if the weather cooperates." She looked up as James entered her kitchen and quickly assessed the look on his face as unhappy. "James, what's the matter?"

"Nothing to do with this case, I don't believe, so I really can't discuss it. Do I smell cinnamon?"

"You do, and I'll get you a slice. I was beginning to wonder whether you were coming today. You're late!" She moved over to the coffeecake warming in the oven. "Coffee?"

"You know me too well, Lou. Yes, coffee would be fine." James took a seat beside Molly, leaving Sam to lean against the doorway where he could see everything. "And how are you this morning?" he asked Molly. "I see you have your jogging shoes on."

"Great! I took a run this morning around town. It's lovely here."

"Oh? Did your run take you down on Queen Street, by chance?"

Molly shot a quick glance at Sam. "It did. Look; what's going on? You both look like you just came from a funeral. Oh, sorry, Lou; I didn't think."

"It's fine, dear, and I agree—you two look like you've got something on your minds."

"Molly, there was a break-in at Monica's this morning," Sam offered. "She lives on Queen Street, and James says he saw someone who looked a lot like you hopping the fence in her backyard as he drove up her driveway. Is there something you want to tell us?"

Molly turned in her seat to face James as Lou placed his snack down in front of him. "I wanted to tell you, but I figured it would make me a suspect. I stopped by Monica's house this morning to clear the air with her. When I got there, she was in my face about Sam, about my appearance, and about something that obviously had nothing to do with me. She must have been talking about the break-in because she ranted about privacy in a small town, or something like that."

"How did you know where she lived?"

"I did a quick search on my smartphone."

"How exactly did you think you were going to clear the air? There's nothing going on between Monica and me…."

"Exactly," Molly interjected. "I wanted to let her know there were no hard feelings on my part, and I offered my condolences on her dad's death. Really, it wasn't much of a conversation. I was just leaving when I saw the police car pulling up the driveway. I chose to hop the fence in the backyard because I didn't want to get in the way of the police, and that was the only way I saw to avoid getting involved. Monica was actually on the phone with someone—I presumed the police—when I first knocked on her screen door. I overheard her say something about a break-in, so I knew I had come at a bad time."

"So you simply said what you had to say and left?" James hadn't touched his coffeecake.

"That's right. I got the distinct impression she wasn't interested in talking to me anyway."

"What makes you think that?" James was hanging on her every word now.

"Well, she obviously has a *thing* for Sam, and I guess she felt like I was intruding in her would-be romance with Mr. Gorgeous over there." At this, Molly thumbed her finger in Sam's direction.

"Okay, Molly, I appreciate you sharing your impression. I would suggest you not go around Monica Maples' house again, though, just to be on the safe side."

"Oh, I wouldn't dream of it, unless of course she invites me for tea and cookies. Then it would be rude to refuse such a kind invitation." Molly's sarcasm elicited a stifled laugh from both Lou and James.

"Well, now that's settled," said Lou, selecting the light-hearted moment to divert the conversation. "Are you two ready for your adventure? I'll have your picnic ready for you in a few minutes."

Sam and Molly took this as their cue and quickly gathered their things for the day. "Sure, Aunt Lou; anything you fix will be fine with us. I'm going to run upstairs for a raincoat—looks like I might need one."

"Sam, I may want a word with you later," James called after Sam. "And Molly, I hope you'll be staying in Edenton a little longer." The edge in his voice was subtle, but apparent.

Raincoats and picnic basket in hand, Sam and Molly loaded the Mustang. Sam helped James load the cabinet in the back of his truck and secured a tarp over it to protect it from the few raindrops that were starting to fall. Watching as Lou handed James boxes filled with memorabilia and tokens brought the other evening, Molly and Sam did their best to get away as quickly and quietly as possible. As Sam drove his Mustang out of Edenton's downtown district and into the country, he quizzed Molly further.

"Okay, off the record now, Mol. What were you doing at Monica's house?"

"Just what I said, Sam. Monica was throwing a temper tantrum. I don't think all of it was due to my being there, either. When I asked what had happened, she told me to mind my own business and invited me to leave the premises or she'd call the police. When the police showed up minutes later, I think she was pleased with her little show of force."

"Maybe James would buy your story, but I'm thinking there's probably more to it than that. Want to start again?"

Molly sighed. "May the sky's clouds fill Monica's open house days with…."

"Cut it out. What happened? For real, this time."

Molly shifted in her seat so her back was to him. After a few seconds, she turned to face him. "Okay, okay. I admit it; she got to me. I didn't like the way she was stalking you. I decided to face her, to tell her to back off. I did look up her address on my phone, just like I said. Then I jogged by her house early this morning, expecting just to talk to her. Her car was still in the driveway. As I approached the house, I noticed the door to the porch was open. I stuck my head inside and knocked on the doorjamb, but the radio was on so loud that I guess she didn't hear me. I let myself in. I called her name again, and again there was no response. I heard water running, so I figured she was in the shower. I was about to leave when I noticed a yearbook open on the coffee table. Curiosity got the better of me, and I lifted the book so I could see which school it was. When I put it back down on the table, the page must have turned over. I swear that's all I touched."

"What about the letter?"

"If it were in there, I didn't notice it. I heard the shower cut off and dashed out the door the same way I had come. I continued on my run and kept going all the way to the marina about a mile away, hoping to give Monica time to make herself presentable. When I jogged back by her house, her car was gone. I continued my run on the street behind her house, thinking I might try her at her office. When I got back to the intersection nearest her house, I saw her car zoom past me and turn into her driveway. I headed back to try to talk to her again. By the time I got up the driveway, she was on the phone. We had the few unkind words between us, and then like I told James, I didn't want to get involved when the police car arrived."

"Honest?"

"Completely." Molly hesitated. "Except for possibly one little detail."

"Molly!" Sam's aggravation tinged his voice.

"Well, James said Monica said she returned home to feed her fish."

"So?"

"When I glanced at the fish tank the first time I entered her living room, there was already fish food floating. You know, those little flakes that float on the surface for the fish to enjoy?"

"Yeah, so?"

"So Monica lied to James. Why did she go back, if not to feed the fish like she said?"

"It's her house. Maybe she decided she'd prefer a different outfit."

"Or maybe she'd prefer a different alibi."

CHAPTER TWENTY-TWO

Pulling into the driveway of the cannery property, Molly leaned forward in her seat for a better look at the horde of people swarming around the dilapidated building. Wielding paint brushes or hammers, four men attacked wooden slats on one side of the building while another three were up on the tin roof patching holes. Two women, who were holding ladders, turned to wave at the car, a look of recognition washing over their faces.

"I recognize them from the other day," Molly said as they pulled to a stop near the main entrance. "These are Harvey's employees, right? Looks like they aim to keep it standing and open."

"Looks that way," Sam answered. He waved at a man who was approaching the car. "Hey, there! Remember us? We're staying with Lou…."

"Yes, I remember you," said Gus. "Your Lou's kin. Bet you didn't expect to see this, did you?"

"It's a bit of a surprise. What's your plan, Gus?"

"Mr. Harvey was good to us. A bunch of us decided we should keep the cannery open in his memory. People will come back—they always do. This community will still support us. We'll make it work."

"Where did you get the money for these building supplies? Must have set you back a bit."

"We all pitched in what we had. A few of the neighbors out in the country pitched in, too. It's always been the best place to get fresh seafood in town. Mr. Harvey's death don't change that."

"Did you talk with Lou about it? She owns it now."

"No, we haven't done that, but I'll ask the committee how they want to handle it."

"Committee?"

"There's a bunch of us that's been talking about buying it ourselves. But if Lou was to keep it open, well, that would probably be okay. We just want to consider all our options."

"And have you considered what you're going to do if Lou decides to sell out?" Molly joined Sam and Gus, her eyes darting back to the driveway as she spoke.

"So what am I gonna do, wait on tables? Make beds in some hotel in Elizabeth City? Clean toilets? No, ma'am;

I'd rather clean fish like my family's been doing for generations. I may be too old to go out in the boats anymore, but I ain't too old to stand here and clean 'em the best way they been cleaned."

"He's right, you know," one of the ladder-supporting women chimed in. "The second a developer comes in and knocks this old place down for condos or some fancy hotel, that's the second we are all reduced to minimum wage. We haven't seen that figure since we first came to work for Mr. Harvey. We can't support our families on that. No way. No one can."

"Mr. Harvey did us right," said Gus, repeating his earlier sentiment. "He was good to us all. And we aim to keep this place going because of his kindness. This community will support that. They know good people, and Mr. Harvey, he was one of them."

Sam looked at Molly, noting the pleading look on her face. Shrugging, he called, "Okay, where can we help?" Caught in the frenzy of keeping a developer away was the easy part. Actually doing so was another matter. As he climbed a ladder to help with the roof, Sam silently recounted the many places in Wilmington and Southport that fell under the influence of developers.

From his vantage point, Sam saw them first. Lester Crouch headed a small parade of trucks in his white Suburban. Emerging from his car, he and his entourage started talking in hushed tones when he saw Sam. "Is Lou here today? Oh, wait. My bad—she's unable to leave the confines of her house," Lester smirked. "Are you her…agent?"

Sam climbed down the ladder, noting all work noise had stopped and the former employees of Harvey Bishop were edging close to hear the ensuing conversation. "I suppose you could call me that. What do you want, Mr. Crouch?"

"Son, you know what I want. This land, and all it has on it. But until the matter of the will is settled, I thought I'd come take a look at *my* fleet of boats bestowed upon me by the late Harvey Bishop."

"Look, you know this place will fail if there are no boats to bring in the seafood."

"Yes, as a matter of fact, I do!" Lester was positively gleeful. "And when that happens, I bet selling it to me won't seem so offensive an option. I'll offer a fair price. And jobs. There will be *some* jobs available. I want to continue to be a good community member, you know. Now if you'll excuse me, I want to see about my boats." Lester nodded his head just as the first drops of rain started to fall. He walked toward the river where a ragtag fleet of boats rocked gently on the water.

A hushed chorus of voices rose in protest. "What kinds of jobs is he talking about, Gus?"

Sam jogged after him and voiced their concerns. "You're going to keep the place open? Like it is?"

Lester Crouch turned around to face him. He looked at the unkempt property, its river docks, the building's broken windowpanes, and rusty doors that he knew opened to the warehouse where pipes circulated river water into giant holding tanks of fresh fish. "If it were mine, it would be slightly different. There would still be a fish market, of course. If it were mine, I'd extend and expand the docks for more pleasure boats and outside seating. There would be a café with good food and drink over there." He motioned to his right, closest to the existing structure. "And over here, I see a row of waterfront townhomes. We'll have to make some improvements to the land, of course, and that all has a fairly steep price tag. I've already met with folks from the state and have started the necessary paperwork for Lou. She truly won't have to do a thing to get it going. Except," he smiled at the thought, "sell the property to me. Like I said, I'll make a reasonable offer. I'm sure she could use the money."

"How much?" Gus sauntered over. "How much you going to offer her?"

"A competitive bidder, perhaps?" Lester clapped his hands together.

"Maybe. If Lou is going to sell, then I may want to buy."

"Whoa, you two," Sam said. "Lou's not said one thing about selling, so Lester, if you have to take your boats, then take them. Gus, if you don't mind, go find the keys to the boats. The rest of the property is not for sale, as far as I know."

When Gus walked out of earshot toward the building, Sam got in Lester's face. "Do you know how hard they've worked here? This is what they know. They don't want it to change."

"Change happens, always. People have to be willing to change, or life is just going to pass them by. Now take me, for instance. I'm willing to change. If Lou's not going to sell the property, I can take my boats and sell 'em. These people will have no jobs without the use of the boats. If, on the other hand, Lou wanted to sell the property, I could be persuaded to lease my boats for some of the boys to go out and get fish for the market. I am a reasonable man, Mr. McClellan."

"So you keep saying."

"Here's the thing. If she's not going to sell, what's she going to do with this place? She's probably not interested in running it the way it has been run all these years. I dare say she's going to get out in the boats herself, you know what I'm saying? And if by some small miracle these good folks here *could* raise enough money to buy it, they'll run it into the ground without proper business managers. Sure, they could always go buy another boat, but the current business model is broken. Look at this place. Can't you see that? At the very least, you have to admit this place is more of a tear-down than a tourist magnet. I could make it something special. I could turn it into a *destination* that would extend Edenton's popularity from the downtown waterfront up into this county. Everyone would benefit."

"Not everyone," said Molly, who stood nearby, her hands on her hips. "I've seen this before. You're talking like your some knight in shining armor, someone who's going to swoop in and fix all that's wrong with the place, but what's really going to happen is a different story, isn't it, Mr. Crouch? You're willing to take away jobs from the people who made this place what it is, what it has been. When you finish with your swank development, there won't be room for these people anymore. Oh, sure, one or two will get jobs standing behind the *market* counter, but the rest? They can just kiss their livelihoods goodbye. What do you think they'll do then?"

"That's not my concern, dear girl." Gesturing to his entourage to follow him to the river's edge, Lester Crouch signaled the conversation was indeed over.

"Arghhh, he's so aggravating! I can see why Harvey wouldn't leave him the property. He knew exactly what would happen to his employees. Sam, you have to do something!"

"What exactly do you think I can do? He has every right to those boats, and what he chooses to do with them is his affair."

Gus returned with the boat keys. He handed them over to one of Crouch's men, who ran to the docks to give them to Lester. He and his men inspected the boats as best they could under their large black umbrellas.

Gus walked dejectedly back toward Sam and Molly. When he reached their position, the skies opened up and the downpour quickly put an end to the work crew's efforts. "This is a bad omen," Gus said, crossing his arms over his narrow chest.

Sam ushered Gus and Molly to the shelter of the building. The rest of the workers followed them inside. "Look; don't give up hope. He only owns the boats, now. Not the building. We can help you find some other boats. I'm sure there are plenty out there that would work. And you know Aunt Lou's not going to sell to him."

"Appreciate it if you talk to her on our behalf. Ask her what price she'd sell it to us for, and I'll take it to the committee. Will you do that for me?"

"Sure. I'll ask her. Where can I get in touch with you?"

Gus wrote down a number on the back of a fish list and handed it to Sam. "We'll be waiting to hear. This place, well, it means a lot to us."

"Got it," said Sam. "Can we help with the repairs? Maybe there's something we can do inside until the rain lets up." He looked around at the holding tanks. Some stood empty, their water stagnant.

"Only if you know how to repair the water pumps. We can't use those tanks without circulating water in them. We've just barely been keeping them working. Mr. Harvey was going to order some new parts, but...."

A smile spread across Molly's face. "It just so happens I can."

"What?" Gus and two others said in unison.

"We have some spare parts in the trunk of the car for a project we did on Sam's boat the other day. I'll go get what we have, and we'll make it work." Dashing to the car, she grabbed her rain slicker and a box of spare pump parts, plus what tools she could grab.

"Don't mind her," Sam answered Gus' unanswered questions. "She's a wizard with all things mechanical."

Moments later, Molly had one of the old water pumps apart on the counter and was installing this and that until she proclaimed it was finished. Reinstalled, the pump started circulating the water.

A small cheer went up as bubbles rose to the surface. Their celebration was cut short by Lester Crouch and his men sticking their heads in the door. "We're going to have to wait until the rain breaks before we can move *my* boats. I'd appreciate it if you all were neighborly and kept an eye on them. I've inspected them so I know what needs to be repaired when I return."

Sam felt as much as saw Gus move toward Lester with a speed Sam didn't think Gus had in him anymore. Sam reached for Gus' arm to hold him back.

"Mr. McClellan," said Lester, "please give my regards to your aunt. I'd like to call on her soon to talk about the offer. Perhaps tomorrow?"

"I'll let her know you stopped by, sure." Sam's tone was flat. He released his grasp on Gus' arm, and Gus stood firmly rooted beside him.

"Very good," said Lester. "Come on, men. Time to get back. I think there's a beer with my name on it." He left the building followed by his entourage under a canopy of umbrellas.

"He's got a lot of nerve," Molly said. "May a thousand flying fish leap into his boat and sink it his first day out on the water."

"I don't think flying fish particularly care for the river water, Mol," Sam said with a smile. "Nice sentiment, though." Turning to Gus, he said, "We'll see what we can do about getting some other boats."

"Thanks," Gus said. "I'm not sure how we're going to manage all this without Mr. Harvey. We'll have to sort it out." He turned on his heels to head back to his friends before spinning around. "Thanks for your help here. It means a lot to us that you'd come help us."

"Wish there was more we could do. I'll talk with Lou about keeping the place open. I'm sure she isn't interested in selling, especially not to Lester."

Gus nodded. "Appreciate that." He and his friends got back to work tidying up the fish-cleaning stations inside while rain pounded the building.

Sam and Molly headed out into the rain and raced toward the car. "We need to do something, Dude," Molly said after a time. "I have lots of friends in the boat business. I can see about finding a boat for them to keep them going. Think they could get a loan?"

"Don't know. Sometimes, Gus seems confident they can pull this off, and at other times, not so much. I wonder…."

"What?"

"We need to speak with Lou. I don't have any idea what she's got in mind for the property—don't think she's really had any time to digest the idea that it's hers now."

"Here's a thought," offered Molly. "What if she'd sell the property to Gus and his friends? Then they could take out a second mortgage on the property to buy the boats? Lester could just have his old boats, and Gus and his friends could continue to do what they have always done."

"That might work," Sam pondered as he pulled into Lou's driveway just as the rain let up. "Let's see what Lou has in mind."

"Aunt Lou?" Sam called as they entered the house. "We're back." He didn't hear anything from Lou's sitting room. He looked upstairs and called again. "Aunt Lou?" There was no response. "Wonder where she went? It's been raining; plus, she's not supposed to leave the house, and her car is still here," Sam said.

Molly shrugged her shoulders, then glanced out the window to the backyard. "The shed door is open. Maybe she's tending to the honey or the bees."

Sam and Molly walked to the shed and opened the door wider as a few stray bees flew by. "Aunt Lou!" Sam cried out. Lou lay on the floor, a small puddle of blood running from her bruised temple. Sam raced to her side and checked her pulse. "She's alive—looks like she fell and hit her head, though. Better call 911, Molly."

"Already on it," said Molly as she punched numbers into her phone.

Lou roused. "Ow. My head."

"Just rest for a minute," Sam said. "Help's on the way. What happened, Aunt Lou?"

"I'm not sure," she replied slowly. "I came in here to check on the honey jar supply so the boys could go get whatever's needed before the next canning season. I was on that step stool checking the inventory like I always do. The next thing I know, my head is spinning and here you are."

"Sounds like you blacked out," Sam said, dabbing the cut on her head with the edge of a paper towel he found on a shelf. "Have you had enough to eat today?"

"Oh, yes, I eat all the time," Lou chuckled to herself. "I must have slipped. I'm okay; no need to make a fuss over me."

"I think we better let the experts be the judge of that," Molly said as she hit *send* on her phone. Moments later, the sound of sirens could be heard racing down the street. "Just sit still until they get here. They will want to check you over for fractures. Can you tell us anything else, Lou?"

"Like I said, I came out to check on supplies. The boys who help me are heading to Elizabeth City this afternoon, and I wanted to be sure I had everything I need before we start up honey season again. I was standing on this stool," Lou pointed to the tipped-over stool at her feet for emphasis, "and the next thing I know, you're standing over me."

"Was anyone else in here with you?" Sam quizzed.

"No, I was in here alone," Lou said. "Although…" she hesitated.

"Although what?"

"I thought I saw someone looking in that window, just there." She pointed to a window on the side of the shed closest to the back of the yard. "I must have been imagining things, though. How silly of me."

The emergency medical technicians ran to the shed with gear in tow. Lou tried to wave them off, but they would not be mollified until they took her blood pressure (which was normal), her temperature (also normal), and asked her a few questions about her general health.

While the technicians cared for Lou, Sam walked around the shed and searched under the window. Thanks to all the rain that morning, he was able to identify the imprint of two shoes. Taking a measurement and making an estimate of size, Sam rejoined Molly and Lou just as the technicians were packing up their gear, convinced that Lou was okay or at least strong enough not to be escorted to the hospital.

"Could you tell who it was you saw at the window? I mean, could you tell if it was a man or a woman?"

"No, no, it was more of a feeling I had that someone was there, watching me. Does that make sense?"

"Perfect sense. Lou, you probably shouldn't go outside without Molly or me or James at your side for a few days—just to be sure you're okay."

"Oh, Sammy, I'm perfectly fine. I just got a little dizzy. Well, hello, James; what are you doing here? You're a little late for lunch."

James Bradley stood in the door of the shed, taking in the scene. "I heard a report of possible trouble at this address, so I came as quickly as I could. What's going on?"

"Nothing, James. I slipped and fell off my stool. I hit my head, and Sam and Molly called for help. They are just leaving, if you need to ask them, but I'm as fine and as ornery as ever," Lou chuckled.

"You need to be more careful, Lou," James scolded. "You could have broken something. Sam, why did she black out?"

"The medical techs said she must have stood up too fast." Sam nodded in the direction of the door. "Can I talk to you outside?"

"Sure." James followed Sam outside to the window on the back of the shed. "What's up?"

"More like what's down. Those footprints are too large for Lou's, but too small for a man. Tell me about the two guys who work for her from time to time."

"Oh, they are good guys, to be sure. Both as big as horses, though. Their feet wouldn't be that small. We'll make a casting and dust a bit to see what we can find." James walked back to his patrol car to get his investigation kit.

I don't think you'll need to look too far, Sam thought. He didn't voice what was on his mind, but he was starting to wonder.

Sam and Molly hung out around the house that evening to wait on Lou, help which she accepted begrudgingly. After Lou turned in for the night, Sam shared his thoughts with Molly. "There were footprints outside the shed."

"One of her helpers?"

"No, too small. I'm thinking Monica may have stopped by unannounced and startled Lou. The thing I can't figure out is why she'd come around."

"Maybe she wants to buy the property? Who knows? You going over there to ask her?" Molly's voice was tainted with emotion that Sam suspected was jealousy.

"Not yet—there's no proof that she was here. Besides, she's like a damn octopus."

That brought a smile from Molly. "Extra-long tentacles, huh?" Molly wrapped her arms around Sam for effect.

"Absolutely," Sam whispered, kissing Molly lightly on the lips. "Time to turn in?"

"Absolutely," Molly mimicked him as he pulled her up from the couch. Climbing the stairs, she asked, "Do you want me to go with you to see Monica? Just for moral support, you know."

"Perhaps. Let's wait to see what James finds out first." Sam closed the door quietly so as not to disturb Lou.

CHAPTER TWENTY-THREE

The next morning, Lou was up early proving she was feeling fine again, and reclaiming her rightful place in *her* kitchen. Soon after James left from his daily breakfast visit, Lou had an unexpected visitor.

"Good morning," Lester called loudly from the porch as Sam opened the door. "Said I'd be by today, and here I am. Where's Lou?"

"Look; she took a bit of a nasty fall yesterday. Could we give her a few days' rest before you start in on her?" Sam's temper was short.

"Now before you get all upset, I just wanted to present her with a fair offer for the property." He puffed up his chest. "May I please speak with her? I'll only take a few minutes."

"It's not really a good time," Sam said, but Lou put her hand on his shoulder.

"Really, Sam, I'm fine," Lou said. "Please let him in."

"Thanks, Lou," Lester said as he followed Lou and Sam into the living room adjoining the kitchen. Molly joined them as soon as she heard Lester's voice.

"I won't take up much of your time," Lester said as he took a seat on the couch opposite the chair Lou chose. "I'm sure your nephew has mentioned to you that I spoke of my interest in the property yesterday. I would like to buy it from you, Lou, and I promise to keep as many of the people on as I can."

"I've not had a chance to discuss our conversation with her yet," said Sam, holding up his hand. "Can't this wait?"

"Actually, it can't," Lester replied. "I thought if we could work something out, I could skip getting the lawyers involved. I really don't want to go through that hassle, and I think it would be in your best interest, Lou, if we didn't have to drag this through the court system. You know Harvey owed me money. That cannery of his was a great big hole—he cared more about the people working there than he did about running the business, if you want to know the truth of the matter. He should have closed it years ago, but he kept it open for their sake. He always talked like I was a business partner as well as a friend, so naturally, we never put anything in writing as I continued to loan him money on the property."

"Naturally," Sam imitated Lester.

"Anyway, I thought it would be best for all concerned if I just present my offer—which is fair, given how much effort and time I've got in that place, and in Harvey, for that matter." Lester didn't waste any more time. Taking an envelope from his shirt pocket, he added, "This is fair price for that land."

Lou took the envelope and slowly opened it. "I find it amazing that you can put a price tag on your friendship with Harvey," she said quietly.

"Well, I am a businessman, Lou. He's got no use for it now."

"And you have big plans?"

"I do indeed."

"Will you keep the cannery open?" Lou asked.

"I'll keep a part of it open, only it's going to become a market with all the latest hot gourmet items tourists and folks like to enjoy after a day of sailing or boating on the river. The downtown docks at the waterfront have only so many slips for boaters. I'm planning a marina that will accommodate twice that many. I want to build condos, too, so there's a need for a market that can support the residents and visitors I expect we'll get. It will be a wonderful addition to the Edenton tourism trade."

"Interesting. And what about Harvey's current employees? Have you talked with them? Is this what they want?"

"I don't think it's their place to decide, Lou. We people with money have to make these decisions. We have the power to transform lives as well as property here. I'm sure the Chamber of Commerce will be delighted with my development proposals. I've been working with an architect to sketch out some plans. They are pretty rough at this point, but they'll do to convey the ideas I have for that property. If you'd like to see them, I can go get them. They're out in the car."

"There's no need, Lester," Lou said as she folded the offer and carefully placed it back in the envelope on her lap. "I don't need to see them. The land is not for sale."

"Lou, think what you're saying!" Lester was on his feet.

"I've thought of nothing else since the reading of the will. It was clearly Harvey's intention to keep that place open, so that's what I intend to do. Thank you for stopping by," she said as she rose. "Sam, please escort our guest to the door."

"But there were other developers he was talking to, Lou. There were two big ones from out of town, in addition to me. I should have the first right of refusal on that property." Lester's voice was on the rise. "Won't you reconsider?"

"Now, Lester, we've known each other a long time. You know me well enough. When I make up my mind, it's set."

"You're going to regret this, Lou."

"No, I don't think I will." Lou walked through the back hall toward her room. The matter was closed.

Sam escorted Lester to the front door and followed him out onto the porch. "Sorry, big guy. Maybe you had your beer a little early yesterday."

"Huh?"

"The celebration with your comrades, remember? You left the cannery in search of libation, as I recall."

"So?"

"So your search didn't by chance bring you by this house, did it?"

"What are you saying? I haven't been here to the house in years. Lou and I knew each other, of course, but we didn't socialize beyond the occasional chamber function. What are you suggesting?"

"Nothing. Just wanted to be sure I had all the facts straight."

"Facts? What's your problem? You saw me at the cannery, and now you see me here. If you have anything to say to me," he pulled out a business card, "feel free to contact me—or better yet, my attorney." Lester Crouch stormed off the porch.

Returning inside, Sam found Molly and Lou in the kitchen. Lou was tending to a kettle of water while Molly was setting cups on the counter and hunting for a box of tea. Sam was amazed Lou was allowing anyone into her kitchen. "That's settled, then."

"With Lester, anyway," Lou said, as she poured a cup for Sam. "Molly's just presented a wonderful idea about Gus and his friends buying the business."

"Would you be willing to do that?"

"Of course! I have no use for the business or the property. And I wouldn't ask much of a price, if that's a worry for Gus. He's been so kind, and I know Harvey thought the world of his employees. They would be the best employee-owners for the property. Sammy, would you be a dear and find Gus to let him know I'd like to sell it to him?" She scribbled notes on a piece of paper. "Give him this. I'll be happy to act as the financier, of course."

"You may want to think about how to restructure the business model so it earns its keep," Molly said. "If what Lester said was true, the business as it was wouldn't be able to stand on its own two feet."

"That's a good point, Molly," agreed Lou. "I don't have any idea how Harvey ran the business, but I know he took good care of his people. That part I wouldn't want to change. But I'm open to suggestions. What would you suggest?"

"Well, I don't want to insult anyone...."

"You love insulting people," Sam quipped.

"Oh, hush, you. What I mean is, I don't know what management skills Gus and his team might have, but if you could suggest they go to a business class or two so they can learn to run the business on their own, that would probably be wise. Another thought would be to hire a local manager and an accountant so Gus and his friends can do what they like to do, which has to do with the fish."

"Good ideas, Molly. How did you get to be so smart?" Sam elbowed her.

"Smart-mouthed is more like it," she laughed. "I've had my fair share of close encounters of the business kind, delivering boats up and down the coast for a living. I still have to keep up with the business side of the house. It's a pain to keep up with the accounting, but since I like to eat, it's necessary."

"Okay, sounds like a good plan. Is there a community college or a small business center nearby?" Sam asked.

"Yes, one of each," answered Lou. "Here, I'll take whatever Gus wants to offer, but this way, he'll have options to consider. Molly, could you help by writing down some of your ideas?"

Throwing around a few more ideas, Molly took notes on a pad of paper she found lying nearby. "If Gus has questions, I'm happy to help," she said when Lou indicated she was pleased with the collection of thoughts.

"Sam, be a dear and take this to Gus. He may be up at the cannery, still."

"Absolutely, Aunt Lou. You got it." Sam put down his cup and headed for the door. "Molly, you want to come along?"

"Naw, Dude, you go ahead. I think I'll stay here and keep Lou company."

Thinking it would be best for Lou to have someone to watch over her, Sam headed back up to the cannery, hoping Gus and his work crew were still at it.

Gus and his friends were milling around by the building, sorting out the day's tasks as Sam entered the cannery's driveway. When Gus saw Sam's car, he waved and shouted, "Morning!"

"Morning, Gus. Guys," said Sam, returning the wave. "I have some good news for you. Lou said she'd like for you all to buy this property. She's willing to do an owner-financing arrangement, so you don't have to worry about a bank getting in the way of things."

Gus smiled. "Wonderful news! We been talking about this, you know, how to make it work. I'm sure the property is worth a lot of money, though…probably more than we can afford."

"She doesn't want the money, Gus; she wants for you all to run the business—maybe get a little help on the management side of things, but you can run it how you want. No developer necessary." Sam handed Gus the piece of paper that Molly and Lou drafted as he explained the terms.

Gus was speechless as he looked over the paper. After a time of passing the paper around to his friends, he quietly asked, "She'd do this for us?"

"Yes. She knows you'll take good care of the place. You might want to take a course at the community college to learn about running a business, and you'll need to think about hiring a bookkeeper. Other than that, you'll get to continue what you've always done."

"I'll have to talk it over with them, but we could do this. We could make this work," Gus said, motioning to this friends. "Tell her thank you for me, will you?"

"Absolutely, Gus. I'll let her know she can expect to hear from you soon." Sam smiled and walked back to his car, feeling good about his small part in helping Gus and his friends. Driving back to town, he focused on Lou's predicament and the bee carcasses left in Harvey's room the night of his death. The lab should be done soon with its analysis; then Lou could be free again. But would she be safe? Thoughts of the unidentified footprints outside her shed worried Sam. *Have to check with James to see what's up with that.*

Moreover, Sam wondered about Molly. He'd been able to trust her in the past, but breaking into Monica's house? That was not something he would have expected her to do. But if it produced results, he could live with it. And the missing letter? Did Molly take it? If she did, surely she would have told him about it. That letter might be something worth investigating, but to do that, he'd have to talk with Monica again—something he didn't want to do without James around.

Before heading back to Aunt Lou's, Sam wheeled into the police station's parking lot. With more questions than he had answers, he needed input from James, and not in front of Lou or Molly, this time.

CHAPTER TWENTY-FOUR

"Good morning—oh, you're that detective." Annabelle's niceness was short-lived when she recognized Sam entering the police station's reception area.

"And good morning to you, Ms. Withers," Sam replied, a smile still on his lips. "Is James Bradley in?"

"He is, but he's not at his desk right now. He's in a meeting."

"I can wait. His desk is…this way?" Sam pointed through a glass door to an open room of desks.

"It is, but I'd prefer you wait right here until his meeting is over."

"Ah, but I see a coffeemaker in *that* room, so that's where I'll be." Sam made his move through the glass doors before Annabelle could move from her reception desk. He wandered through the desks toward the coffee station, spying name plates on desks until he found one with James' name on it. Grabbing a cup of coffee, Sam took a seat at James' desk and sifted through files on his desk until he found one marked, *Maples*. Sam knew he'd only have a minute before Annabelle would squeal on him to James or summon security, so he grabbed the file. Inside, he found a report and pictures of Monica's living room. Indeed, there was one of the fish tank, and fish food flakes hugged the water's surface, just as Molly said. *Why would Monica lie about that?*

"See anything interesting?" James approached his desk. An amused look played on his face. He raised his hands to indicate Sam could remain in his seat behind the desk, and then he took the seat opposite Sam.

"Not really," Sam said. "I was just wondering about the letter that supposedly went missing. What was the significance of that letter? If it was so valuable, why keep it in a yearbook? Doesn't seem like a logical place to stash something special to me."

"Who knows why women do what they do? Anyway, we don't know if that's the place it always was, or if Ms. Maples was just reminiscing."

"Maybe another conversation is in order?"

"Look, Sam; this is local police business. My chief is on my case enough as it is, noting that I've shared a lot of information with you that I shouldn't be. He came down hard on me in the staff meeting a few minutes ago."

"Meetings. Bleh." Sam made a face to show disgust. "I remember them well. I can step aside anytime you want me to, James. Just trying to look out for my aunt, you know."

"I am too, Sam. And I think you'll be pleased to note we heard back from the lab today. Seems your girlfriend was right. The bees found in Harvey's room were indeed African." He pulled out a file from his portfolio case. "Let's see—here. There were positive matches. The carcasses were at least two months old, so they were planted."

"So Lou was framed."

"Afraid so," James said quietly. "Question is, who would do this?"

"Someone who had no idea about what was in Harvey's will. Someone who stood to gain a lot if there wasn't anyone there to inherit his wealth."

"Or property," James added. "I'll send a car for Lester. Time to get him in for questioning."

Sam leaned back in the chair to the point of tipping. "Sounds like a plan. I'll go tell Aunt Lou the good news."

"Okay, Sam. Tell her I'll be around in a bit."

"Will do. Thanks." Sam left, but not before saluting Annabelle on his way out the door.

Sam walked up the street to the real estate office where he saw Monica through the window. Though she was on the phone, she held up her finger to suggest she'd only be a minute longer. Soon, she hung up the phone and met Sam on the street. "I didn't think I'd see you again."

"I was hoping we could have a cup of coffee. Across the street?"

"Sure, I can take a short break. Is your…friend going to join us?"

"Molly? No. I wanted to talk to you alone."

"Hmm? Well maybe we should go back to my house."

"No, the coffee shop will be fine." Sam noted Monica's face change, but he didn't comment. "It won't take long. Promise."

"I wouldn't mind if it did," Monica said as she wove her arm around Sam's while they walked across the street to the coffee shop. "But have it your way."

When they were seated with coffee in hand, Sam began. "Monica, I understand there was a break-in at your house. James was kind enough to share that with me since I'm here helping Aunt Lou for a while. Are you missing anything?"

"Just a letter. It was something I treasured from Harvey. I had it out the night before, and I had tucked it in the back of my yearbook before I went to bed. After the break-in, it was missing. I can live without it—I'm sure it has no value to anyone but me, but it's what little I have of the man who was my father."

"That, and his books," added Sam.

"Yes, I've got to make time to get them all out of the house, but there's still yellow crime scene tape across the porch. Whenever I get the chance, though, you could come by to help. I could use a little brawn." She edged closer to Sam.

"Maybe I can help. Sounds like lots of stuff to move. What are you going to do with the books?"

"Don't know. Now that Harvey's dead, there's really not much reason for me to stick around. I figured I'd sort through them and donate what I don't want to the library or something." She hesitated. "Such a waste."

"What's that?"

"Well, his house, his business, his books. Disposing of the books is the easy part, and the rest of the trouble falls to your dear aunt. If I had inherited the house and the business, I'd know exactly what to do with them. The house needs some freshening up, of course, but it would fetch a good price if left in the right hands. And that business? Well, it's a tear-down in its present condition."

"I suppose you'd want to develop it into condos or something?"

"Makes sense. That's what people want these days. They don't want to take care of lawns in a resort town. They want to play." She purred her last sentence suggestively.

"I'm sure Aunt Lou will sort it out in her own time. She's grieving, you know."

"I suppose we all do that in our own ways."

"This is going to sound odd, but did you stop by to visit with Aunt Lou yesterday?"

"No, of course not," Monica said in a flat tone. "Why on earth would I do that?"

"I don't know, to…talk about things like the real estate, maybe?"

"No, I'm sure she will…as you say, sort it all out. I'm sure she can do that without my help."

"Agreed, I just wondered if by having a conversation with her, it would help to clear the air. You seemed so tense at the reading of Harvey's will. I thought perhaps you were, well, really upset."

"I was, but not at Lou. I admit I felt Harvey should have remembered my mother, and by way of extension, me. I had hoped we'd formed at the very least a friendship since I came to town, and that he would feel, oh, I don't know…."

"Obligated?"

"Well, yes, why not?"

"So you have no ill feelings toward Lou."

"No!" Monica took another sip of her coffee. "This is sounding a little like an interrogation, Sam. I appreciate your interest in my feelings and all, but I am beginning to wonder if there's something else on your mind."

"No, just that you mentioned seeing the yellow crime scene tape across Harvey's front porch, so I figured you'd driven by there and perhaps stopped to talk to Lou. I'm just trying to help, Monica; that's all."

"Well, it's not helping me." Monica's tone was icy. "If that's all, I suppose I should be heading back to the office—

unless you'd care to continue this conversation over lunch at my house."

Sam smiled. He could guess quickly where that would lead, if Monica had her way. "I'll have to pass, Monica."

"What's the matter? Afraid Molly won't understand? She came by my house to visit me, you know. I wondered if she broke into my house, but she claimed she knew nothing about a break in. She wanted to tell me to stay away from you, I believe. Ironic, isn't it, that you can't seem to stay away from me, and she's insistent that *I stay away from you*?" Monica put her hand on Sam's arm. "You know, you haven't asked me out sailing yet."

"Yeah, about that," Sam started. "I—"

"She really likes boats," Paul's voice boomed from the doorway, interrupting Sam.

"Oh, hello, Paul." Monica removed her hand from Sam's arm and sighed.

"Hello, beautiful. And hello. Sam, right?"

"Yes, Sam McClellan. Nice to see you again, Paul. Look; I was just about to leave. You can have my seat, if you like." Sam rose from the table despite the look of displeasure on Monica's face.

"How thoughtful of you, Sam. Monica, it's just like old times, you and me having coffee in the mornings." Paul winked at Monica. "I stopped by your office and they said they saw you walk this way. I was hoping you could come be my crew this Saturday—last week's race was rescheduled, and it looks like the weather is going to be great for a change."

"I don't know; Sam has offered to help me remove books from Harvey's house, and I was thinking Saturday would be the best day to do that."

Sam looked at Paul and then at Monica. "Well, we didn't have a firm commitment or anything. The house is still considered a crime scene, so it would be up to the police to say when you could get in there. Maybe Paul could help, too—it will make the job go that much faster."

"Great idea," Paul said. "I'll swing by to pick you up for the race on Saturday evening; then after we win, I'll help with the move if the police say we can get in. Now that's settled; back to work for me."

"Where do you work, Paul?"

"I work in economic development."

"So you're downtown?"

"Yes. Edenton is a great place—you can be across town in minutes. And when will you be leaving?"

Sam noted the edge in Paul's voice. "Haven't decided yet."

"Well, let me know when you're leaving, and we'll have a party in your honor." Paul slapped Sam's back just a little too hard for Sam's liking. "See you later, Monica."

"Right, Paul," Monica said. As soon as Paul was out of earshot, she turned back to Sam. "Now see what you've done? I'll have to go sailing with him again."

"Sorry—I thought you'd want to crew for him in the last race. You seemed keen on it for last weekend."

"I prefer to make my own decisions, thank you very much." Monica stood up, smiled politely, and headed for the door. Sam waited a few minutes, then walked to the police station to get his car.

When he got back to Lou's house, Sam was greeted at the door by Aunt Lou. Her car was nowhere to be seen. "Hi, Aunt Lou; where's your car?"

"Oh, I let Molly take it. She said she had some errands to run and that she'd be back tomorrow."

"What kinds of errands would keep her away over night?" Sam wondered whether Molly had somehow managed to drive by the coffee shop and seen him and Monica inside.

"She didn't say. She said she'd be back, and since she's with you, I know she's trustworthy. She'll bring back my car."

"Well, I thought you might like to use it yourself."

"What?"

"The bees were planted in Harvey's room, Aunt Lou. James will be over in a bit to go other what details of the case he can, but for now, just know that you are a free woman."

"Oh, Sammy, you've done it! You cleared my name. Thank you!" Lou's eyes welled up with tears. "But who killed Harvey?"

"That's not yet been determined, but I'm sure we'll get to the bottom of it soon enough. James told me to tell you he'd be over here soon."

"Come in and have some lunch. Did everything go okay at the cannery? What did Gus and his friends say?"

"They are putting their heads together about their offer and terms for you. I bet we'll hear back from them soon."

"What a relief. I know they will do a fine job with the place."

"Speaking of places, what will you do with Harvey's house? You'll have to wait until the police say you can do anything with it, but when that's over, what will you do?"

"I have no use for two houses in town. Most likely, I'll sell it, but I haven't really had time to think about that, yet."

"Whatever you decide, I'll help with what I can." Sam thought about his sailing timetable for a split second only. Lou needed his help, and he'd stay until he was sure she'd be okay without him there.

"That's so kind of you, Sammy. I don't want to interfere with your plans, but I will say I've enjoyed having company here the last few days or so. And now, with my name cleared, I guess I should start making plans again."

"Plans?"

"Yes, Sammy; once the cannery is taken care of and Harvey's house is sold, I think it may be time for me to visit your father. He's the only family I have. This matter with Harvey has made me realize just how fortunate I am to have family. Harvey thought he was alone—well, he was, for years and years. To learn he had a daughter, well, he did the best he could with that news and tried to include her in his life. I sensed she was not pleased about the will, but truly, she shouldn't have expected much more. She looks like she can manage on her own, anyway. No, I think it's time for me to bury the hatchet with your father once and for all. The matter was so trivial, after all. We inherited property from a distant relative decades ago. He wanted to sell, and I didn't. He badgered me daily until I finally blew up at him. Looking back on it, it would have been wise to sell. The property's not worth the riff it caused between us. I've been considering moving to Raleigh, or maybe somewhere near there to be closer to him if he'd be okay with that."

"I'm sure he'd be more than okay with that," said Sam, hugging her gently. "Do you want me to call him?" Sam moved toward the kitchen's phone.

"No, not yet—I have to figure out what to say, first." Lou smiled. "We have a lot of ground to make up."

"Okay. Well, if you don't mind, I'd like to call Molly." Though he was thinking it, he didn't add, *to see what she's up to now.*

"Sure, sure. Why not use the phone in the other room? I'm going to serve our plates, and we can eat in a few minutes."

Sam's repeated calls to Molly's phone went unanswered. *Wonder where she went?*

After lunch, Sam decided a stretch of the legs would be good. He needed to go check on his boat anyway. "Think I'll take a walk this afternoon, Aunt Lou. Unless you have something you need me to do around here, that is."

"No, you go on. All this excitement has made me tired. I'm thinking I'll try for an early nap this afternoon. Take your house key so you can let yourself back in, Sammy." After washing the lunch plates, Lou adjourned to her room and closed the door.

The heat was up this time of the day. So were the bees, buzzing around late-blooming flowers. Walking down Oakum Street toward the waterfront, Sam veered off a side street that took him back through the Mill Village, past the condos, and down to the edge of the cypress swamp. Swatting at ever-present mosquitoes, Sam looked forward to getting his boat back out on open water too far from shore for the little bloodsuckers. For now, he'd have to put up with them, though. He climbed into his dinghy and rowed back to *Angel*.

Once aboard, he checked all the lines, the anchor, and opened the hatches to allow some of the day's heat to escape. Something was not right with this case, he knew. If the bees were a plant to frame Lou, then whatever it was that killed Harvey had similar poisonous properties that induced anaphylactic shock. That could have been any number of venoms, or cocktails made to look like something else. Besides the poor repair job on the screen in Harvey's bedroom, there were no signs of forced entry. A friendly visit leads to an assault? Surely, Harvey would have seen something like that coming. And if it did happen that way, why did such a malicious visitor feel a need to exit from the window, using the stacked books as a ladder? Back to square one.

After a thorough review of all of *Angel's* systems, Sam locked up. He rowed his dinghy back to the town docks at the edge of the waterfront, then headed over to the lighthouse for a quick tour. Paying the admission fee, Sam entered the small wooden structure overlooking Edenton Bay. As a sailor, Sam appreciated the exhibits that told the story of the lighthouse keepers who had lived here as well as how the lighthouse had been moved ashore. Sam also noted how much of the Albemarle Sound could be viewed from the lighthouse's perch. Walking back down the ramp to the park, Sam saw a familiar figure heading his way: Monica.

"What a coincidence, Sam," she purred. "I was just on my way home, and I always take an evening stroll around the park—I do it every day about this time to work off whatever naughty things I've eaten for lunch—and here you are! I do so enjoy bumping into you."

"Yeah, what a coincidence," Sam answered.

"Look; why don't you walk me home? After the break-in, I'm a bit jittery about being there all alone."

"Did the police find anything?"

"No, they are still working on it. I think they have much bigger fish to fry since, in their eyes, nothing of value was stolen. I am sure with you there, I'd feel *much* safer."

"Okay," Sam answered. "I can walk you home, but wouldn't you rather have Paul do that? He's been your significant other and all—shouldn't he be your hero?"

"Oh, shhh. I'm not interested in Paul with you in town. I keep telling you we could have a good time, and you keep trying to pawn me off." Monica pouted. "Don't you like me, Sam?"

"I like you just fine, Monica, but like a told you before, I'm involved."

"I know, with that *Molly.* I'm not sure what you see in her, really."

"To each his own, right?"

"Be that as it may, and under the circumstances, I'd really appreciate an escort home tonight. You could check things out for me and then leave. I won't tell if you won't."

"I could do that. Are you ready to go now?"

"Yes, I'm done for the day."

"What about your car? Don't you need to drive home?"

"I leave it at the office sometimes and walk the two blocks for exercise if I don't have showings or errands to run." Monica smoothed down her skirt for effect. "Here, we'll walk in this direction." She pointed toward a path that led from the lighthouse to the far edge of the park.

For a split second, Sam's mind played the "what if" game. What if Monica really was in danger? What if Harvey's murder and the break-in at Monica's house were related? Worst of all, what if Molly came back to Lou's earlier than expected and found Sam gone? It wouldn't take her long to find the dinghy at the waterfront park once Lou told her where he'd gone. No, walking Monica home wasn't the brightest idea he'd ever had.

"I noticed your boat looks a little lonely out there in the cove," Monica said, pointing toward *Angel*. "Maybe before we go check out my house, you could take me aboard. I'd love to see what you sail. What type of boat is she?"

"An old Morgan," Sam said, ignoring her expressed interest in a tour. "I've been fixing her up over the years. This is the first time I've really had a chance to do something other than work all day and just live aboard her. In fact, it's the first time I've been cruising. Always wanted to, but work, life, stuff…well, it all got in the way."

"So you're out for an adventure. How exciting! Where will you go next?"

"Virginia. To Norfolk, to see my son." *No harm in telling her that.*

"Are you going to ask me to sail away with you?" Monica teased as she slid her arm through Sam's.

Knowing she wouldn't quit this line of reasoning any time soon, Sam changed the subject. "Seems you and Lester have a lot in common, since you're both in real estate."

"Lots of people are in real estate. This is a small town, but there's enough business to go around. Lester and I don't really run in the same circles, if you know what I mean. He's a bit of a bully, from what I gather, and I prefer the strong, silent type—men of action, rather than words." She stroked his arm while closing the already small gap between them.

"I guess that's what it takes to be successful in the real estate business these days—being able to talk his clients into buying or selling."

"Oh, it's not that hard," she said. "If I listen closely to what my clients are after, I can usually find a good fit for their needs. For me, it's a win-win situation. I get what I want without being a bully."

Sam turned to Monica. "And what exactly do you want here in Edenton, now that Harvey's dead?"

"Aside from you?"

"Aside from me."

"Well, closure, I suppose. We've talked about my disappointment, so perhaps it's best for me to focus on what comes next." Monica led Sam up the driveway to her cottage. "You'll have to excuse the mess," she said as she opened the back door. "I've started packing."

"For what comes next?"

"I have a friend in Charlotte who is subletting her apartment to me until I find a place of my own. There's not much to pack up here. I left much of what I own in storage before I moved to Edenton. I suppose you do the same?"

"Nope. Everything I own is on my boat. I don't really have a need for anything else."

"You're kidding, right?"

"No. I never had the need for *stuff.* That kind of life isn't for me."

"Wild and free? I like that. I wish I could be more like that."

You seem to have the wild part down pat, Sam mused, but he thought better of saying it out loud. "Let's check to make sure nobody's been visiting you today."

"You mean like a perpetrator returning to the scene of the crime?"

"Yes, something like that." Looking in closets and in the bathroom, he toured the small cottage in minutes. "Looks like you're safe. I don't see any signs of disturbance anywhere."

"Oh, Sam, how can I thank you for checking on me? Makes me feel safe and…tingly all over that you would care enough to walk me home and peek around for intruders. Truly gallant."

She's a bit melodramatic and over the top for me, Sam thought. "Well, now that we know you're safe, I'll be heading home." Sam purposefully walked through the kitchen toward the door.

"Just one drink?" Monica hinted. With a hand on his shoulder, Monica gently turned him around. "I promise, nothing more. Scout's honor." She reached into the refrigerator for a bottle of wine. "There's something I want to talk about," she said as she opened the cupboard for glasses. "I suppose I should have told the police this, but I would feel better if I could talk to you about it first." Monica took her time pulling a wine bottle out of the refrigerator and uncorking it like a grand production. "It has to do with Harvey's death."

Boom. Sam felt obligated to hear her out. He took the glass of wine she offered him and waited for her to replace the stopper in the wine bottle.

"Let's sit in the living room," Monica offered. When they were seated (a little too close for Sam's comfort), she began. "I've not been entirely up front with you about Lester."

"I'm listening."

"When I first got to town and he found out that Harvey was my father, he was on me in a hurry. It's a small town, so it quickly got around who I was. Anyway, he approached me numerous times to see if I could help him get what he wanted out of Harvey. This was before Harvey died. They had a bit of a falling out over money, I guess. I can imagine Harvey wasn't flush with cash whenever Lester came around looking for payments on what he constantly called his *loans* to Harvey. It was clear to me that he was pretty mad about the length of time it was taking Harvey to pay back what he owed, and I guess Lester felt I had some kind of sway over Harvey, being his daughter. Lester asked me on several occasions to speak on his behalf to Harvey."

"And did you?"

"I wasn't sure how to bring up the subject. Besides, it really wasn't my place to get in the middle of their business dealings since I wasn't around to be privy to their earlier conversations about loans or property."

"Why didn't you tell this to the police?"

"Keep in mind what I said earlier—about his being the town bully."

"Did he threaten you?"

"Not outright, no. But I wasn't sure how serious he was about the unkind remarks he made about my...father. Sounds odd to call Harvey that, after all this time of not knowing him."

"Like what?"

"Well, he said things that made me uncomfortable. He said he hoped he'd get his money out of Harvey before he died, and that the cannery land was worth a fortune if only

Harvey would let someone else do with it what should have been done to it a long time ago."

"Did you ever hear him threaten Harvey directly?"

"No, but like I said, I was never in the same room with the two of them to hear their conversations. Lester could have threatened him—sometimes, he acts irrationally, if you ask me."

"Okay, well, tomorrow, you have to go to the police and tell them what you told me. I have no jurisdiction in this town…. I'm not on the case, not even a police officer anymore. You'll have to deal with the local force."

"Oh, Sam, I just can't. What if Lester comes after me to retaliate?"

"The police will protect you once you tell them the whole story. You know you can get in a lot of trouble for withholding this kind of information, don't you?"

"I didn't really think it was all that important, until after Harvey…Dad died. And with the break-in here, well, I think it's gotten me all jittery and nervous."

Funny; you don't seem like the nervous type. "It's important, all right. You need to talk with them. Is there anyone in your real estate office who can corroborate what you're saying? Someone who was around in the office whenever he showed up? Maybe someone who overheard what he was saying?"

"I don't know. I can ask around in the office tomorrow. Most of the time, he seemed really cautious about what he was saying and where we were talking. Like, before he would speak, he'd look around to see if anyone could hear him. He even came to my house once or twice."

"If that's the case, you have to find someone in the office who overheard him. Did he ever call you? Your phone's call log could prove he called you, though not what was spoken. If we needed to, we could…or the police could…track that down on his phone, too."

"Yes, I can share my phone's log. There were several phone calls before Harvey died."

"Any after that?"

"Only one that I remember. That time, he was calling to offer his condolences and to say that he was sorry for some of the things he'd said earlier."

"Was this before or after the reading of the will?"

"Before, I think. I can check the date of the call to be sure, though."

"You'll have to. The police will want to know. Sounds like you have a lot to share with them that will help with this case. Do you want me to walk you to the police station this evening? I'm sure they'd like to get started."

"No, Sam, I'd rather do it in the morning. It's getting late, and I have a busy day tomorrow, what with work, showing houses, and now this trip to the police station."

"Okay, but promise me you'll take care of it first thing?"

"Scout's honor."

Scout? "Good. Now I'll leave you alone so you can get your rest." Sam got up to leave.

"I'd love to have some company tonight, if you can spare the time. We could just…visit." Monica was back on the prowl as she followed him closely to the door.

"Thanks, Monica, but I really should call it a day." Sam waved goodbye and was out the door before Monica's long talons could set in his back. He felt like running away, but he maintained a steady pace down Monica's driveway. Cursing himself for not insisting she go to the police immediately, he decided he needed to escort her to the police station right then. He was just two houses away when he saw Lester's car turning into Monica's driveway.

For a second, he thought about going back to Monica's, but he felt certain the local police should be involved rather than him running to Monica's rescue. They'd hauled Lester in once already; maybe this would be the break they needed. Jogging to the police station, Sam found the front desk manned by a junior officer. He explained the situation and left. The police would be able to handle it without him interfering. Plus, he wouldn't have to be the consolation prize for Monica after they finished.

CHAPTER TWENTY-FIVE

Steaming coffee mug in hand, Sam watched from the safety of Lou's front porch as police marched in and out of Harvey's house the next morning. From the looks of things, they were doing another sweep of the crime scene.

James was with them, having stopped by Lou's earlier for a cup of coffee and a bite of coffeecake. He had said that the investigation was going smoothly, but that Lou was no longer a suspect in the murder of Harvey Bishop. Lou, of course, was relieved, but a little put out that she'd been a suspect in the first place.

"Morning, Sam!" Molly called from Lou's car as she pulled in the driveway. "What's going on next door?"

Sam stood rooted for a moment before walking to the car to help her unload a suitcase. "Another round of hunting, looks like. And where have you been?"

Molly smiled broadly. "I had to check on the progress on my boat. The yard called yesterday and needed me to approve some upfits to *Hullabaloo*. It wasn't something I could do from here. Besides, it allowed me to get a few more of my things. Miss me?"

Sam pulled her close in a hug and kissed her on the cheek. "More than you'll ever find out."

"Oh? And just what did you do last night?"

"Aunt Lou and I hung out," Sam lied. When he had returned to the house the night before, Lou had already turned in. "Nothing much. Here, let me help you with your bag." Sam grabbed a small suitcase out of the trunk and carried it up the porch stairs. "What's in here, bricks?"

"Laptop. I wanted to keep up with things on my boat's restoration, so I brought this back to check emails. I need to line up the next delivery to pay for the yard's work. What did I miss while I was away?"

"Lou's no longer a suspect," Sam said. "James can probably shed more light on the details, but the lab confirmed what you said about the bees."

"Who would want to frame Lou?"

"Still working that one out. James hauled Lester in for questioning, but released him. I don't think they had anything to stick just yet."

"Yet?" Molly was sharp. "What do you know that the police don't?"

Sam pursed his lips. He didn't want to have this conversation with Molly, and he was hoping James would finish his tour of Harvey's house quickly so he could be the bearer of the news. "It's just a hunch, Mol. Look; here comes James," Sam said, relieved to see James walking across the yard toward Lou's house. The three took a seat on the porch.

"Morning, Molly," James said. "You missed a bit of excitement around here while you were gone."

"So Sam tells me," she said. "What's this about Lester being your prime suspect now?"

"We've had a talk with him about a few things. This morning, Ms. Maples stopped by the station on her walk into work. Seems he's been harassing her, and according to her, he previously made veiled threats against Harvey. She said she would like to have us keep an eye on him for her safety."

"My, my," uttered Molly. Seeing Lou coming to the doorway, she jumped up to help Lou with a tray of coffee mugs and hot scones.

"Morning, Lou," James said. He stood and offered her his seat. "Help you with that?"

"No, no, I'm fine. What were you saying just now?"

"Monica Maples has come forward with information about Lester that puts him in sort of a bad light," Molly offered.

"Oh, dear. Why on earth would Lester want to harm Harvey? They were friends for years and years," Lou exclaimed.

"Something changed, Lou," offered James. "We're not sure what, but we'll get to the bottom of this. A car's gone around for Lester. We have enough against him to hold him now, given what Monica's said."

"It's not proof, though," Sam was quick to add.

"No, but it's a start." James inhaled a scone and reached for another. "You've outdone yourself with these, Lou."

"Thanks, James. I think I've lost my appetite, though. I just can't understand anyone wanting to hurt Harvey, especially Lester."

"He wanted more than he was getting back, I guess." James trained his efforts on a second scone.

"Did he have any idea what was in the will? I thought that was privileged information. You know, lawyer confidentiality and all that," Molly said.

"Jackson indicated Harvey had changed his will several times in the weeks before his death," Sam said. "Maybe Harvey suggested to Lester somewhere along the way that the changes he was making wouldn't favor Lester. Would that be reason enough for a falling out?"

"Only Mr. Jackson could tell us what was in the earlier wills, and that's going to take a subpoena. Well, guess I better be getting to it. This may take a while, given how things work. When I left, Lester was screaming from his holding cell. We could hear him throughout the entire office. If I didn't have to come over here for another look-see, I probably would have made another excuse to leave."

James stood up. "This is the best excuse ever. Lou, as always, thank you for the treat and coffee. I hope you won't mind if I continue to stop by, even though I truly don't need to check on you for your police purposes anymore."

"I'd be offended if you didn't, James," Lou said with a smile. "You're welcome here anytime. I also want to tell you I appreciate your faith in me, even when others in this community turned their backs on me."

"No need for that, now, Lou. You all enjoy the rest of your day. Looks like I'm going to have a full one. Hmm, Sam, could I talk with you for a minute?"

"Sure, James." Sam followed him out into the yard. "What's up?"

"Did Ms. Maples tell you anything else when you visited with her last night?" James hushed his voice so Molly couldn't hear just the short distance away from where they stood.

"Oh, she told you, huh? Yeah, she said she'd feel better if somebody checked out her place. She said she was concerned about being alone, though I'm not really sure she should ever worry too much…she seems like the kind of girl who can take care of herself."

"She is that," James said wryly. "Did she give you any more information about Harvey and Lester's dealings?"

"Not much more than what you've already told us." Sam rubbed the back of his neck, feeling the weight of Molly's stare. If she found out he had been with Monica, even as innocent it was, she'd be gone again for good. "She claimed Harvey didn't talk to her much about business dealings, and I guess the subject of Lester didn't come up. Lester wanted her to talk to Harvey about the loans he'd made, but she said she didn't want to butt in. The only thing she did say was that when Lester came to visit her in the real estate office, he was acting 'cautious'—like he was afraid someone was listening in on their conversations. That struck me as a bit odd. Lester doesn't seem like the cautious type."

James laughed. "There's not a cautious bone in that man's body. He rages around town like a bull in a china shop most times."

"I gathered that. Monica said Lester was a bit of a town bully."

"You could certainly consider him as such. How long were you there?"

"Not very long. Let's see; she approached me in the park shortly after she got off work, we walked to her house, talked a bit, and then I left. I'd guess it was around seven o'clock when I left her house."

"And she didn't come after you? She didn't call you, or talk to you after you left?"

"No, she didn't. I came directly to the station to let the guy on the desk know what Monica had said, and that I saw what I thought was Lester's car pulling into her driveway. Did he tell you why he was there?"

"Just said he had come to talk with her about another real estate deal they were both involved in. Ms. Maples confirmed that part of the conversation. She said she'd asked him to leave about the time we showed up, so if there was more going on, there couldn't have been too much to it."

"Is there anything else?"

"Not that I can think of right now. I'll call you if I need anything else. Are you staying on at Lou's for a few days more?"

"Yeah, I can do that." Sam started to walk toward the steps before James called him back.

"Sam, if you hear anything else, please let me know."

"Of course, James. You can count on it." Sam stopped, cocked his head to the side, and waited two seconds before speaking. "You look like you've got something else on your mind. What's up?"

"I really would like to bring closure to this matter, but some things are just not adding up. The cards are stacked against Lester, with a motive of the land grab. Too bad for him Harvey changed his will one too many times in his last few weeks of life. Hopefully, Jackson can shed light on that one. The trouble is Lester's alibi on the night of Harvey's death is air tight. He was out of town, and has the hotel receipts to prove it. What's more, he's screaming at me that it was Monica who kept asking him—pushing him, actually—to ask Harvey to sell the cannery land to *her.*"

"So it really will boil down to what Jackson shares with you. Does Monica have an alibi for that night?"

"She does—she was with her sailing buddies on a boat. Big race or something. We confirmed she was on the boat during the time of death, having a good time."

"Oh, yeah, Paul. She told me she was crew for him, though I got the distinct impression she wasn't too keen on him."

"That's not how he tells it, but okay, a girl can change her mind, I suppose. We cleared him to come get Harvey's books for her once this mess is over. We're just doing a final sweep to see if we can find anything else, but we have reached a dead end over there. We've dusted everything, and no unusual prints; nothing else out of place besides the bees."

"Is anything the matter?" Molly called from the porch.

"No, Mol; we're done here," Sam answered for James. Turning to James, he said, "Call if I can help with anything."

"Sure thing, Sam. Thanks again, Lou," James said, waving goodbye before returning to Harvey's house to finish up for the day.

"What was that all about?" Molly asked Sam as he sat down beside her on the porch. "Is there a break in the case?"

"Actually, no. Lester is locked up for the moment, but the police are still working through the loose ends."

"Lester, Lester," Lou said softly. "All for a piece of land. What a shame." She wiped away the tears that started down her face.

"Now, Aunt Lou, don't get yourself worked up again. The police will resolve this. You're not in any danger. And we'll stay with you as long as you like, won't we, Molly?"

"Of course," Molly said. "I can stay for a bit longer before I have to run a delivery up the coast. The snowbirds get anxious this time of year. Trying to beat hurricanes and all. And, of course, I can always come back when I finish."

"No," Lou said, shaking her head. "No, you both have lives to lead. I appreciate what you've done for me, and the company has been grand, but don't wait around for me. I'm sure I'll be fine. It's just going to take a little while to get used to life without Harvey. Will you please excuse me?" Lou got up and stacked coffee mugs on the tray. "I'm going to go lie down for a bit."

Sam held the door for her, and then he returned to Molly on the porch where she was pulling her laptop out of her suitcase. "What's that for?"

"Something I came across while I was waiting on the boatyard yesterday. Remember I told you I was curious about the yearbook on Monica's living room table?"

"You mean when you were snooping?"

"Oh, be quiet. I turned it so I could see the cover. Well, I did a little research. Once I figured out what year I was looking for, it wasn't too hard. So much information is online these days. Seems Monica Maples had a dear friend—very close in age, in fact. They were often mistaken for twins. Here, look." She turned the screen so Sam could see a bookmarked page of images from a yearbook. "Different names, but they look identical."

Sam read the names under the pictures. "Same mom, different dads?"

"Don't know…. I found the obit for Monica's mom—that part of her story was definitely true. She did die of a heart attack. Though according to the obit…wait, I've got it here." She opened another computer window. "Take a look. Monica and her mom were estranged. It's not in the obit, but if you read between the lines, and cross-reference with these other articles I found, you can see references to relationship struggles."

"What do you mean?"

"One of the best friends from the high school yearbook moved away, while the other stayed close to home in Charlotte. See? This article shares more details about the good works Monica's mom did in the community with her daughter at her side. And this article shows the prodigal daughter returning to a hero's welcome of some sort."

"What did she do to deserve that?"

"High school reunion—she came back."

Sam read the short article about the high school reunion. Who was there, what they wore, and what they did for the three-day event. Special mention was made about the people traveling the farthest to get there, and Natalie Jefferson won the prize. A fairly recent picture showed Monica and Natalie hugging each other. They look just like sisters, to be sure. "Any idea where Natalie is now?"

"According to this article, she calls Thailand home these days." Molly opened up another bookmarked page and shared the screen again. I don't know if that's of any significance to the case. I thought it was interesting, though."

"Was it worth breaking into her house to find out?"

"Maybe not, but I was curious. There weren't any pictures around the house that I saw."

"I think she intended for this to be temporary. The house is really tiny, and she doesn't strike me as the shabby-chic cottage type."

"Oh?"

"She's already packing up."

"And how would you know that? I didn't notice any moving boxes when I was there."

Sam hesitated. "James told me. He said he want to get this solved quickly because he felt it needed to be closed. He mentioned seeing boxes on his last visit to her house."

"Is she a flight risk?"

"She's not officially a suspect, so she's free to come and go as she likes."

"I see." Molly's forehead clouded with lines.

"Molly?"

"Yes, Sam?"

"I don't want you to go near her. Let the police take care of this."

"Yes, Sam."

"I mean it. Until we know for sure what happened, you don't need to go near her or the house again."

"Sam, don't you see? She was in Harvey's house. She used the books like a ladder to climb out the window. She somehow managed to get the bees because she wants to throw the police off the trail."

"How do you figure?"

"Woman's intuition."

"She had an alibi, Molly. Miss Monica Maples was accounted for at the time of Harvey's murder."

Molly closed her laptop and looked thoughtfully at Sam for a moment. "And all alibis are water-tight, right?"

"Come on, Molly; James knows what he is doing. He has witnesses that place Monica on a sailboat in the middle of the Albemarle Sound at the time of Harvey's death. If anyone here has a lousy alibi, it's Lester. He can't prove where he was that night. Everything points to him: he had the motive, he had the means, and he had the opportunity."

"Anyone with sense could have gotten the means—African bees can be found online. Besides, the bee carcasses were old—James said the lab confirmed it. I agree, he had motive. Greed over money? Just how much did Harvey owe him? Nothing was in writing, and he didn't say, so I'm guessing that it was a lot. I guess you're right. It just seems too...convenient."

"Well, convenient or not, he's behind bars now," Sam said as he rose. "Want to go get some coffee downtown?"

"Sure, but before we hit the java, I'd like to see if we can get in to talk with Lester."

Sam sighed. "You really think that's a good idea?" He walked down the porch steps behind Molly, who struggled to walk while pushing her laptop back in her backpack.

"I just want to see him. He may feel like talking, you know?"

"Molly, this is police business. They have to wrap it up, not us."

"Since when are you a spoil sport? I'm just thinking about Lou—I want to be sure she's safe when I leave."

"Leave?" Sam stopped two steps behind her. "I thought you weren't in a hurry."

"I said that for Lou's benefit. If she truly needs me to stay, I will. But I have to get some deliveries in soon before hurricane season, Dude. This is the most lucrative time of the year for me."

"Oh."

"What's wrong?" Molly stopped at the sidewalk and turned to face Sam.

"Nothing, Mol; I had hoped you'd be able to go sailing with me for a few weeks before you had to head out again. That's all." He pulled Molly close and kissed her on the cheek.

Molly kissed him back. "It'll just be for a few weeks—I have to get the snowbirds' boats out of the islands before November. Can I get a raincheck?"

"Sure," Sam said. He squeezed her hand while he tried to hide his disappointment. "Now how about that coffee?"

They walked quietly down Oak Street and turned on Water Street. Taking in the view of the vast Albemarle Sound, Sam thought briefly about setting sail again. *If Molly isn't able—or interested—in sailing with me now, I guess I could take off anytime. Aunt Lou doesn't seems to need me to stay.*

Approaching the police station, Molly pointed out the boats at the waterfront docks. "Looks like a good crop there today. Will you move your boat closer to town for provisioning next? I can help before I go, if you like." It was as if she could hear Sam's thoughts.

"Yeah, probably a good idea. I'll start provisioning tomorrow. There's no reason to stay in Edenton as long as Aunt Lou is okay."

As they entered the police station, Sam and Molly could hear the unmistakable booming voice of Lester from a holding cell. They approached the reception area where Annabelle greeted them with her usual frown.

"The chief isn't in, so you might as well turn right around." Annabelle made an exaggerated circle with her finger, indicating she wanted them to leave.

"We're not here to see him. We'd like to talk to Lester for a minute, though." Sam leaned on the top of the reception station and smiled the brilliant smile that often allowed him to get whatever he wanted—or so he thought.

Annabelle wasn't impressed. "That's not going to happen, either. He needs to have his lawyer present for any police questioning."

"I'm not on the force anymore. Besides, I just wanted to see how he was getting along in your fine establishment today."

"He's doing as well as he would anywhere," she said in an exasperated tone. "Can't you hear him bellowing? He's been at it all day!"

Molly jumped in. "Oh, so he's a difficult guest?"

"Annabelle, this is my friend, Molly. We were just on our way for coffee—could we bring you some?" Sam tried to be cordial to see whether that would get him anywhere.

Annabelle straightened her shoulders and pursed her lips into a straight line. "No, thank you. I have had enough coffee already today. Pleasure to meet you, Molly."

"Likewise," Molly said, reaching over the counter to shake hands with Annabelle, much to Annabelle's surprise.

It was clear from the way she arched her head back that *no one* was allowed in her personal space. She shook hands with Molly, then quickly squirted hand-sanitizer on her hands in protest of the intrusion.

"So you were saying Lester is difficult?"

"Lester is difficult anywhere he goes. That's just the kind of person he is." Annabelle smoothed her hair as she spoke. Molly took front and center with Annabelle while Sam moved away slowly toward the hallway from which the bellowing was emanating.

"Tell me more about him," Molly urged Annabelle. "Have you known him long?"

"As long as he's been in Edenton. He came here a few years back."

"Oh, he isn't from here?"

"Heavens, no!" Annabelle seemed shocked that Molly would suggest such a thing. "I know everyone in this town. I've been here my whole life, and Lester is certainly *not* from here."

"Do you know about his background? I'm just curious to find out why people do bad things."

Taking his cue, Sam slipped down the hall and found Lester without difficulty. An officer on duty nearby waved at him as Sam approached.

"You're Bradley's friend, right?" He stood to shake hands with Sam. "I'm Sullivan."

"Nice to meet you. Yes, James has been kind to my aunt during this case. I just wondered how Lester's getting along in here. I gather from all the yelling that he's not too happy."

"You could say that. He's not going down without a fight."

"Has he contacted his lawyer?"

"Yeah, he's on the way. Coming from Greenville today."

"That's interesting that he chose not to deal with a lawyer in town."

"Not surprising, though. We have lawyers who deal with real estate deals here—but criminal trial lawyers? That's a bit of a stretch."

"Mind if I talk to him for a few?"

"Be my guest." Officer Sullivan escorted Sam down the hall to Lester's cell. "I can only give you a few minutes. He's going to be moved to the Chowan County Jail in about an hour. They have far more room than we have here."

"That's all I'll need." Standing outside the small room, Sam could hear Lester cursing. As Sam opened the door, Lester glared at him.

"What do you want?"

"Just to talk for a minute."

"I've said everything I'm going to say until my lawyer gets here."

"I've heard you're going to be moved to the county facility today. You sure there's nothing you want to tell me? I might be able to help."

"The only thing I've got to say is the same thing I've been telling them already. I didn't kill Harvey."

"I'm not here about that, Lester. I just wanted to know more about Monica, and I thought maybe you could help me understand her."

"What's the matter—your little girlfriend not enough for you?" Lester's snickering made Sam's stomach turn.

"Maybe," Sam played along. "My friend is about to leave, so I thought I might get to know Monica better. You seem to be pretty familiar with her."

"Not in *that* way, though I wouldn't have minded. She's hot." Lester sat down on the metal chair before continuing. "We met some time ago in Charlotte. She actually approached me at a meeting."

"What kind of meeting?"

"We met at a convention. We were in a breakout session being led by a mixed-unit developer—you know the kind, where there are single-family homes in the same neighborhood as condos. Anyway, this huge company was looking for parcels of land large enough to accommodate its types of properties, and it was offering substantial sums for properties."

"But you didn't own any to take advantage of their generosity?"

"Right. They also offered a hefty finder's fee, and that got my wheels turning. Harvey owed me money, and at one time, he was talking about retiring. I told him many times I'd take the cannery land in repayment for all the money I've loaned him over the years."

"Wonder why he went to you instead of the bank? He had collateral."

Lester laughed. "Harvey didn't trust banks. He was a self-made man who bootstrapped his way up from the bottom. He paid cash for everything...at least when he had it. The last recession hit the cannery pretty hard, so he was considering his options."

"And selling to you was one?"

"Sure. We had a gentleman's agreement, and he said he'd talk to his lawyer about it."

"This was all before Monica came to town, right?"

"Exactly. When we met, she said she might like to visit Edenton, and that it sounded like her kind of place. I thought she was referring to the real estate climate. The market here doesn't suffer in a recession quite the way other small towns do. It's always bounced back sooner since there's the attraction of the Albemarle Sound right next to the colonial town that is frequently covered in national magazines. The town has every imaginable amenity, including healthcare and charm, so it's a mecca for retirees. It never occurred to me that Monica might spoil my plans. We got to talking, and at first, I thought I might have a chance with her. Somehow, though, she managed to connive her way into talking with the big developer and convinced him that she could get her hands on a huge piece of waterfront property. *My property!*"

"The cannery?"

"Exactly. From that moment on, it was a race to get Harvey to formalize our deal and sell me the land."

"But did you know she was his daughter?"

"Not until I got back to Edenton. She was sly. She didn't mention it at all when we met. It wasn't until about a week later that she showed up. And it didn't take her long to get a toe-hold in this town. She got in with the 'right' people, and she avoided me once the news was out about Harvey being her father."

"So you thought you'd be out of the picture if the land was transferred to her."

"Exactly." Lester snorted. "I enjoyed seeing the look on her face that day in the lawyer's office when she learned she wasn't getting the land, either. That just made my day."

"Why did you go to her house the other night?"

"To try one more time to reason with her. She was leaning on me pretty hard to force Lou's hand. She thought if I got her to sell the cannery to me, then she and I could split the proceeds when I sold it to the big developer."

"Makes no sense…unless she felt sure you'd have some reason to share in your good fortune."

"Well…." Lester seemed deflated. "Truth is, she has been threatening me since she came to Edenton."

"What does she have over you?"

Lester sat down on the edge of his cot, signaling their visit had ended. "I'm done talking. I didn't kill Harvey, and I don't have to tell you anything else."

"Fine. You'll have to tell the judge, so I'll hear about it sooner or later. Lester, I'm trying to help here."

"She got in good with the developer, and he was cutting me out of the deal," Lester blurted. "She said I wasn't working it fast enough. The mega-developer was going to approach Lou himself to cut out the middleman, and she'd get the finder's fee. How she managed to wriggle into that, I can only imagine," he added in a sarcastic tone.

Officer Sullivan appeared in the doorway. "Time's up. We have a car waiting for him."

Sam smiled. "Thanks for your time, Lester. I hope it all works out for you."

"I didn't do it!"

"Thanks, Officer Sullivan." Sam walked back to the reception area where Molly was getting an earful about Annabelle's family's place in Edenton's colonial times.

"Much obliged," Sam waved at Annabelle. "Molly, how about that coffee, now?" Sam moved to the doors to signal he was ready to go.

"Sure, Dude. I'm ready." She turned back to a surprised Annabelle. "Thanks for your time and insight. And thanks for the overview of the town's history. It's lovely here."

Annabelle stood from her perch. She didn't look at Sam, but stayed focused on Molly as she spoke. "Any time you'd like to come back for a visit, *you* are welcome."

Molly picked up her laptop and followed Sam out the door. He noted the smile playing at the corner of her mouth as she walked with him up Broad Street toward Sound Side Acoustic Café. "What's so funny?" Sam asked.

"Nothing, really. I was just thinking how your 'chick magnet' allure had absolutely no effect on Annabelle."

Sam smiled. "I'm good with that." He opened the door to the coffee shop for Molly and followed her inside.

CHAPTER TWENTY-SIX

"So what did he say?" Molly held her questions until after they each had a cup of coffee in hand and were seated at a window-side table.

"That he's not the culprit." Sam carefully chose his words, noting each of the nearby tables in the small coffeehouse was occupied. "He was pointing fingers at someone else, but that just doesn't make sense to me." Sam knew Molly would understand who he was referring to without naming names.

"Because she has an alibi?"

"Exactly. He wasn't kind about any of their dealings, I'll add. He was slow to come around, but it sounds like they've each been putting pressure on the other to bring the cannery land to the table on a big money-making deal. Without the rightful owner's okay, though, it's not going to happen."

"But what about the…." Molly paused and lowered her voice to a whisper. "What about the murder?"

"They each have alibis. Strong ones."

"So there's someone else in the picture?"

"That's what we're supposed to think."

Molly's face clouded. "You don't suppose…."

"I'm wondering the same thing. Can I borrow your laptop?"

"Sure. I need to use the lady's room anyway. Be back in a flash." Molly slid her computer toward Sam and excused herself from the table.

Once the laptop booted up, Sam typed in his keywords and scanned the search results. Reading a few short articles, he found little mention of the name he was looking for… no criminal records, no disreputable mentions, or much of anything else.

"Looks like that's a dead-end," he said to Molly as she approached the table. "What now?"

"We'll find something," Molly said. Just then, her cell-phone rang. "Hello? Yes, this is she. Oh, hi. How did you hear about me?"

Sam tried to follow the one-sided conversation as best he could.

"Wonderful. Yeah, I can do that for you." She quoted a price and added, "You can use the online pay system on my website. I'll call you when I get to Wilmington—I can be there in two and a half hours. Thanks for the call."

"What's up?"

"A sweet delivery. I've been working to line up a regular gig with a company that finds these kinds of deliveries, and I think I may have just gotten my foot in the door!"

"Leaving out of Wilmy? Today?"

"No. The caller said today was the boat tour and the owner interview. They can be pretty picky, so she was offering me a trial delivery at my base rate of one of their smaller boats first. If they like what I do with it, they'll put me on a year-long contract with steady pay and benefits."

Sam's heart fell, but he forced himself to sound happy for Molly. "That's great news. I know you'll do a good job. Where is the boat supposed to be delivered to, and when do you think you'll be back?"

"The boat's heading south to the islands. It's a one-way job, so as soon as I'm done, I can catch a plane back. Maybe I could fly to Norfolk and catch up with you there."

"That would probably work. I want to hang out with Aunt Lou for a few more days before heading out, so I'll reach Norfolk by the time you reach the islands, for sure."

"I love it when a plan comes together," Molly said, a bright smile on her face. "I'm going to head back to Lou's now to pack—I really need to hurry. Don't want to miss this opportunity or the money it represents. Do you have any idea how much full-time captains earn? It's respectable, for sure, Dude. You can hang on to my laptop until I see you in Virginia, if you like. I have my phone, so we can stay in touch." She held up her cellphone for emphasis.

"Okay, sure." Sam stood, too, but he stopped where he was when Paul blustered in the door. "I'll catch up with you at the house. I want to talk to Paul for a second."

"Paul?" Molly turned to look.

"Monica's friend." Sam leaned over and kissed Molly's cheek. "I'll be there in just a few minutes."

Molly waved at him as she brushed past Paul on her way out the door.

Sam stepped in front of Paul before he could reach the counter to place his order. "Hey, Paul, mind if I ask you a question?"

Clearly agitated at the delay of getting his caffeine, Paul snapped, "Now is really not a good time."

"It will only take a minute, promise."

Paul took the seat Molly had vacated. "What do you want?"

"The truth. What exactly is going on with you and Monica?"

"How the hell should I know? She's hot; she's cold. I have absolutely no idea what's going on with her. Frankly, I'm tired of her toying with me."

"What do you mean?"

"Simple. When I saw you two together the other night at the restaurant, she acted as if I weren't there. Then on the boat during the last race of the season, she was friendly, agreeable, and downright frisky. It was like it was when we first met, you know, when she first came to town. I was thrilled, and I asked her what the deal was. She just said she had no idea what I was talking about, and that any woman who didn't see my charm wasn't worth knowing. She added that she 'enjoyed' my company. By the end of the race, I could tell she was really hot for me. After we dropped off the rest of the crew at the dock, we headed back out for a midnight sail. I thought for sure we were together again, if you know what I mean."

"So are you…back together?"

"Like I said, I thought we were, but I just stopped by her office to ask her to come to lunch with me, and she brushed me off again. Like I said, hot, then as cold to me as a Minnesota winter."

"Sorry to hear that," Sam said. "Wonder what caused her to have a change of heart the day of the race."

"No clue. If I ever figure it out, though, I'll let you know." Paul stood. With his eyes on the board over the counter, he squinted to read his choices. "Funny thing about that night," he said, in a lowered tone. "Monica didn't…well, this is awkward, but before when we were intimate, she'd dive in with tons of energy. Almost aggressive. This time, she seemed a little, I dunno, shy."

"Maybe she was tired after a day on the water?"

"But it wasn't a daytime race. It was in the evening. The last race of the season is supposed to be a bit more challenging, so we don't get started until nearly eight o'clock. We only had about an hour of light before it got dark. That's the fun of it."

"Sounds dangerous."

"Yeah, the more beer, the merrier. That's why it's called the beer can or hibachi race series." Paul snorted. "We get the grills lit up on the back rails and grill steaks or chicken, whatever, really. We've had a few close calls, but nobody's died yet. Now, if you'll excuse me, I've got to get my coffee. See ya around." Paul worked his way by a neighboring table to the counter to place an order, leaving Sam with more questions than answers.

Opening up the laptop again, Sam reviewed the bookmarked articles Molly had shared with him earlier. He read Monica's mother's obit. Molly had done a good job, even if she was fishing in the wrong pond. Or was she? He read it a second time, noting the date of Monica's mother's funeral. Scanning the rest of the obituaries in the Charlotte newspaper around that date, Sam's eyes locked on one in particular: an obit of a man ten years his senior who drowned while diving off Australia's Great Barrier Reef. It was the last name that struck Sam. *Jefferson*. Going back over the bookmarked articles, Sam found the one that triggered a gut ache. Natalie Jefferson was his widow…Monica's best friend and doppelganger. Sam instantly felt sick to his stomach.

Sam searched the last week of the local paper's reports and found what he was looking for: an article detailing the small craft explosion and lone unidentified female boater whose charred remains were in a lab waiting on an identification match. Sam had to find Molly. She had been right all along. It wasn't Monica on the boat that night of the race with Paul, but Natalie.

Slamming the laptop lid shut, Sam bolted out the coffeehouse door and ran the two blocks to Lou's house in search of Molly.

A flood of relief washed over Sam when he saw the car still in the driveway. Taking the porch stairs in one leap, he dashed into the house. "Molly!"

"Why, Sam, what on earth is the matter?" Lou hurried from the kitchen with a towel in her hands.

"Where is she?"

"I thought she was with you, dear. I haven't seen Molly since this morning when she walked off with you. What is the matter?"

"Lock this door behind me and don't let anyone in. I mean absolutely no one. Do not go out this door at all! Do you understand?" Sam shouted. He knew he was alarming his aunt, but he had to make sure she'd do exactly what he said.

"Sammy, you're scaring me!"

"Just lock it and stay inside."

"But I was just about to…."

"I don't care," Sam yelled as he backed out the door. "You do what I say." He ran back to Monica's real estate office on Broad Street only to learn that Monica had told her office mates she was leaving early for the day.

Catching his breath for a moment, Sam looked up. From where he stood, he could clearly see the people sitting at the table in the coffeehouse where he and Molly had sat earlier. Whipping his head around, he saw through the real estate office window the desk where Monica had sat the evening before their first "date." Sitting there, she would have a front row seat to watch everyone—including Molly—come and go from the coffeehouse.

Sam took a deep breath and raced down West Queen Street to Monica's cottage. Monica's car wasn't there, but the back door stood open. Entering cautiously, Sam saw that everything looked orderly, if not staged: boxes sealed with packing tape lined one wall of the tiny living room, while stacks of clean newsprint waited on a table for more packing. Moving through the empty house, Sam noted the lid to the aquarium was up. A puddle of water in front of it with a towel haphazardly thrown on top of part of the water caught his attention. Taking a second to look into the aquarium, he saw plenty of fish. Yet something seemed out of place. A small fish net lay on the table beside a can of fish food, wet from recent use. Sam racked his brain, but he couldn't see what was missing. Heading back out through the kitchen, Sam played *what if* through his options. *What if Molly took a different route—maybe the scenic route down by the water—back home? If she had walked that way, he wouldn't have seen her. But she indicated she was in a hurry, so she would have taken the most direct route. What if Monica had already skipped town? Why would she take the time to pack up this place if she were running away?* He reached for his cellphone to call James. *What if....* His thoughts were interrupted by the sound of a car pulling up in the cottage's driveway. Bolting outside, he was greeted by Monica, who was holding a small gun, a Bodyguard 380, trained between his eyes. Knowing the gun had laser sites for accuracy, he stood still.

"Drop your phone." Monica was as cool as ever.

"It's over, Monica."

"Oh, honey, we're just getting started." She moved around to the passenger side of her black Suburban, leaving the driver side door open. Get in the car. You're going to take me for a little ride. Finally."

"You don't have to do this, Monica." As he got in the car, he saw Molly folded into the backseat, unconscious. "Molly!"

"She can't hear you, dear," she said in a honeycomb-sweet voice as she slid into the passenger seat. While the gun remained pointed at his head, she used her other hand to gesture casually toward a glass jar filled with two inches of water tucked in the curl of Molly's body near her stomach. Inside was the golf ball-sized octopus Sam had seen in the aquarium on his first visit to Monica's cottage. The lid to the jar was nowhere to be seen.

"Oh, and careful. That cute little blue-ringed octopus can get agitated if you drive too fast. Wouldn't want that now, would we?"

The octopus had been a brownish-yellow color that night Sam saw it in the tank in Monica's living room, but today, it looked like its name. "That?"

"Yes, it's a pretty beastie, too, don't you think? They have a nasty bite, though. A venom strong enough to kill. When it's happy, it looks almost like the color of putty. Right now, its feeling a little threatened. Sort of like me, I suppose. The blue rings you see on its tentacles make it look so pretty, don't you think? It packs a wallop for its small size. They start out as little things, about the size of a small green English pea. They generally live in tidal pools or in very shallow waters, so they are frequently the cause of nasty surprises to divers and alas, children, who are excited to touch their first—and last—octopus. Interestingly, as soon as a male mates, he dies. There's some poetic justice somewhere, I'm sure," Monica laughed. "That leaves the females literally holding the eggs in their tentacles for six long months. After that incubation time without food or rest, the mothers die, too, leaving the hatched offspring to fend for themselves. No wonder they are easily agitated. Now drive."

"Where are we going?"

"I bet you could guess if you thought about it."

"The cannery?"

"Bingo! Give the boy a prize."

"Monica…."

"Shh, shh. No talking right now. It makes my little beastie upset." Monica held up her hand in mock protest. "Just drive. I'll tell you more about my pride and joy. It's an interesting creature. Each little octopus hatchling has enough venom to kill up to ten men. The venom is produced by a bacteria that lives in the octopus' salivary glands. The creature has a tiny little beak, and this is how it injects its badness. The venom is much like that of a blowfish's venom, which affects a victim's peripheral nerve impulses. This results in rapidly progressive paralysis of muscles, which isn't good when it finally gets to the lungs that can't contract. Causes a nasty suffocation."

"Or drowning, in the case of a swimmer."

"Exactly, Sam. You're so smart. Oh, and my personal favorite, when a victim's heart muscle can't contract, well, it's the equivalent of a heart attack. You know, anaphylactic shock can lead to heart attacks too, come to think of it."

Sam looked in the rearview mirror and pulled out of the driveway. Making his way slowly back to the main street out of town, he worried about Molly. "Did you use that thing on her?"

"Not yet. She just got a nasty bump on the head when she got into the car."

"You mean when you forced her in."

"Wasn't too terribly difficult. She's so gullible, you know. I thought you'd be with a smarter girl. Like me, for instance. Anyway, she willingly got into the car when I told her poor Aunt Lou had called me, of all people. Your little friend couldn't stand to be left out. Curiosity, and all that."

Thinking Molly was not in imminent danger, Sam drove slowly up the road that led to the cannery. "Is there an antidote for its bite?" He urged Monica to continue talking so he could think of a plan.

"Sadly, no. Victims should be treated as if they've been bitten by a snake: immobilized and kept awake, and an oxygen tank pumping for the first twenty-four hours until the venom wears off. Complete paralysis can occur within minutes of a bite, and the funny thing is most victims won't even feel it when they've been bitten. It's like the small sting of a sweat bee—if only hurts for a split second."

Sam reached the cannery driveway. "Very interesting, Monica. Or, should I say, Natalie?"

"Oh, Sam, you really are too smart for your own good. Now be a dear and pull up by the back door. You and Molly are expected, I believe. You'll have to carry your girlfriend to the warehouse. I just had my nails done, after all."

Sam pulled the car close to the building as expected and parked. Watching Monica…or Natalie, as the case seemed to be, reach for the open octopus jar, he saw no opportunity to attack. He felt helpless as she motioned with the gun for him to get Molly out and carry her inside the building.

"Careful; you wouldn't want to drop her," Monica added.

Instantly, he smelled the gasoline surrounding the door he entered. Inside the warehouse building, he noted gasoline cans lining the floor like traffic cones marking off a construction area.

"There's a bench, just there," she pointed with the gun. "Feel free to make yourself comfortable." As she slid the warehouse door closed, she added, almost as an afterthought, "Oh, Sam, where are my manners? Did you need anything before I leave?"

Placing Molly gently on the bench, he noticed a small trail of blood leading from the bench to a dark corner.

"You'll have to excuse my housekeeping skills. My last guest was a bit of a mess."

"I'm afraid to ask." Sam narrowed his eyes, calculating his chances of taking her out without being shot—or getting Molly hurt.

"That little trail of blood belongs to the late Miss Maples…the real Monica. We are—or were, best friends. Harvey was her dear father, and when I got to town, I called to let her know I'd found her long lost daddy. Of course, before I could make introductions, she needed to do something for me—I had a terrible headache the night of the last race of the season, and I knew Paul needed crew. I sent her in my place. She played along and pretended she was me. She and Paul had a lovely time. In fact, she was almost giddy with excitement when she finally came back to my place. But her being in town created a problem for me. First of all, she got Paul all hot and bothered about having a real relationship. I instructed her just to go out for a friendly sail, and she took it upon herself to mess things up for me. He's been calling daily ever since then, and I just reacted. I suppose I shouldn't have taken it out on her, as she was only trying to help, but I was angry with my bestie. Besides, she quickly would have found out what I'd done."

"You mean she would have found out that you murdered her father? Or that you murdered your husband with your little pet?"

"Perhaps both. Needless to say, she outlived her usefulness to me. As, I'm sorry to say, have you."

"You're not going to get away with this," Sam said.

"Darling, I already have. I brought Monica up here that night after her sail under the pretense of wanting to show her around a bit, and to introduce her to her dear father. It was dark, but she was tipsy. She was so excited to meet her father, and I told her he was up here: he wanted to welcome her to town by giving her a tour of his cannery business. It really was a bit of a dilemma for me," she added. "We had been friends for so long. Care to guess how I did her in?"

Sam thought the woman looked thrilled to share her dirty little secrets. "Let me guess. You whacked her on the head, gave your little critter a chance to leave a mark, threw her in a boat, and managed to blow up the boat way out in the Sound. How did you get back to shore?"

"Don't you remember? I told you on our first night together that I love to dive. I had my air tank, mask, and flippers in the boat. It was a lovely night for a swim. I stashed a change of clothing near the lighthouse. Anyone seeing me walk around the base of it that late at night wouldn't have been the wiser since so many people enjoy that waterfront park at all hours of the day—and night."

"Lester is singing like a song bird in that holding cell," Sam warned, "so it won't be long before the police figure it out."

"Let them try," she cooed. "I'll be long gone before they catch me."

"But you had nothing to gain, once that will was read. Why do all this now?"

"Revenge is sweet, even when it doesn't pay so well," she said with a sly smile. "Pity," she cooed. "I really would have enjoyed having you as my boy toy for a while longer. We could have had so much fun, Sam. Ta." Waving the little jar as she moved through the door, Natalie smiled brightly. Then she slid the door shut with a loud bang.

Sam heard a second thud and imagined another bar being lowered in place to lock them in. Within seconds, the putrid smell of gasoline rose to meet his nose, and he saw that the bench where Molly lay was drenched in it.

Racing to the door they had seconds ago entered, Sam could feel heat climbing its way up the metal. Looking down, he saw a shiny trail of gas from the door to the bench. How could he have been so blind? He started shouting. "Molly! Wake up!" Racing back to her, he shook Molly until she groggily barked, "What do you want?" Trying to sit up, she made a face and then heaved like she would throw up. "That smell! Gas!"

"Yeah, we have to go now." He grabbed her around the waist and helped her to stand. "Can you walk?"

"I think so…. What happened? Where's Monica?"

"It wasn't her. Monica Maples, the real Monica, is dead. Her B-F-F is Natalie Jefferson. You know, from the yearbook. We gotta get out of here."

"You're not making any sense," Molly said as she struggled to sit up. "My head!"

Sam was less than gentle with her. "Molly, we have to go. You need to get up now. Can you stand?"

Molly's eyes fluttered for a second, then opened wide. She covered her mouth with her hand. "I'm gonna be sick!"

"Hang in there—we have to get out now," Sam yelled. Looking up, he saw flames coming in under the door. He helped Molly up and scanned the warehouse. He tried to remember the layout of the cannery. "Come on; the market entrance is over here!" Sam half-dragged Molly with him as flames raced the length between the door and the bench where Molly was only seconds ago. Glancing over his shoulder at the flame-engulfed bench, he noted how drenched Molly's shirt was. "Take it off!" he yelled at her.

"What?"

"Your shirt! Get it off now! It's covered in gas. Here's my shirt." He ripped his shirt off as fast as he could while Molly stripped hers off and threw it backward toward the flames. One by one, the cans of gasoline exploded around them as they ran through the warehouse toward the market door.

"Hope she didn't think to lock the front door, too!" Sam yelled as he burst through the door separating the warehouse from the fish market side, flames close behind. Reaching the glass front door, he picked up a metal trashcan and hurled it at the door to shatter it. "Careful!" He shielded his face with one arm and helped Molly through the mess of shattered glass and flames, racing to get away from the burning building.

"You okay?" Sam held Molly tightly as he ran. With sufficient distance between them and the building, he stopped and looked back in time to see a side of the structure collapse with a gut-wrenching, groaning sound. Plumes of smoke changed the Carolina blue sky to thick black as the orange flames devoured the roof.

Molly nodded through her coughs and tumbled to the ground in a heap. She waved him off when he tried to turn her over to check on her, so he felt that was as good an answer as he needed.

"You stay here—I'll be back for you as soon as I can." Sam ran around to the side of the building. The car was gone. Trying to figure out his options, Sam was jarred from his thoughts by Molly's heavy hand on his arm.

"You are so not leaving me here, Dude." Doubled over again, Molly coughed and raised her hand to signal she needed a minute to catch her breath. "I'm coming with you."

CHAPTER TWENTY-SEVEN

Knowing better than to argue with Molly, Sam helped her toward the dock where two boats stood, seemingly unscathed. Sam chose what he guessed would be the fastest and hotwired the battered old Grady White. As the engine roared to life, Sam quickly untethered the dock lines, bumping into a crooked piling as he backed the boat out of the slip while Molly gathered herself up in a ball on the bench seat behind the center console.

Sam calculated there would be only one right answer, so he willed himself not to play the *What If?* Game, but rather to focus on the river ahead. Moving at full throttle speed, Sam covered the length of the two-mile wide Chowan River quickly before it dumped into the Albemarle Sound at the high-rise highway separating the two bodies of water. The wind felt cold against Sam's bare chest as he rounded the corner into the larger part of the Sound, but he scarcely noticed since beads of sweat rolled down his forehead. Adrena-

line had kicked in long ago and showed no signs of letting
up any time soon.

As he passed the town docks, Sam looked at the waterfront park's lighthouse and thought back to when he first
saw it. Freshly painted, the structure looked serene. Not
at all how he felt at the moment. Recounting how much
time it would take for Natalie to drive back to town from
the cannery, Sam knew he was probably too late. When he
reached the low bridge separating the larger bay from the
smaller cypress forest, he slowed the boat to coast close to
the shore before killing the boat and leaping off. He didn't
wait to watch the boat glide partially under the bridge and
get wedged there, nor did he stop to chat with the gawking
passersby; instead, he tore up Oakum Street to Lou's house.
He didn't wait for Molly to slide over the side of the boat to
make it to shore, either.

He had his hand on the doorknob when he heard a
shriek coming from the backyard. Flying through the
fence, he saw Aunt Lou holding a smoker up to Natalie's
face while she thrashed her arms in an attempt to ward off
the acrid smoke. The jar beside her feet was empty. Quickly
searching, Sam saw the small blue-ringed octopus wriggling
slowly in the grass, its tentacles waving like small snakes.

Sam grabbed Natalie's flailing arms behind her with one
hand and put her in a chokehold. "You okay, Aunt Lou?"

"I am now."

"Thought I told you not to go outside."

"You said not to open the front door! I didn't…. I came out the back! Really, I'm just fine. Which is more than I can say for her." Lou put the smoker on the ground and crossed her arms defiantly.

"Oh, you…you spoiled everything, Sam!" Natalie did her best to kick at Sam.

"It's over. Aunt Lou, go call James."

"An excellent idea, Sam." Lou walked to the house to do as instructed.

CHAPTER TWENTY-EIGHT

James didn't take long dispensing his official obligations. He and Officer Sullivan hauled Natalie away in cuffs just as a fire chief's car drove up in the driveway with a report of the building's condition. At the same time, Molly reached the house.

"You're okay!" Molly ran into the backyard where Sam was and threw her arms around his neck.

"How is the building?" Sam didn't feel hopeful.

"It's a total loss," said the fire chief.

"I don't doubt it. And how about Natalie?" Molly motioned with a thumb pointing back over her shoulder toward the front of the house.

"She's not going to be well for a long, long time," Sam said. "She used a venomous octopus on Harvey, Monica's real dad. I was wondering what a seasoned fisherman would need with a *Beginner's Guide to Marine Biology.* I remembered seeing it on his nightstand. It's almost like Natalie left it as a calling card."

"That's just sick."

"Yeah, you could say that. What's worse is that she used that venomous octopus on her husband on a diving trip—made it look like a drowning. She was trying to use it on Aunt Lou, and she took advantage of the fact that she and Monica looked so much alike to set up her alibi. She had the real Monica go sailing with Paul that night so she could take care of Harvey. Then, after that was over, she knocked Monica off, too. Yeah, I'd say she's going to have lots of time on her hands to think about things."

"Sounds like that little critter of hers is well-traveled," Molly said. "May Natalie Jefferson get stung by a thousand wasps next time she stops to smell the roses," said Molly, passing one of her curses for fun. "Is Lou okay?"

"She's fine. You know, she's a lot stronger than she looks." Sam smiled. He picked up the hive smoker and noted the weight of it. "A lot stronger."

"I don't understand what she could have gained by coming after Lou."

"Revenge. Since she didn't get anything substantial from Harvey, she wanted to destroy everything that was important to Lou, including the cannery."

"And you," Molly suggested.

"Okay, and me. She demonstrated what she was capable of, and she was probably trying to tie up loose ends."

"Big fail," Molly said as she kissed Sam.

"Yeah," he said, kissing her back.

"Come on in, you two," Lou called from the back door. "I've got a chocolate cake here that needs attention."

"Coming, Lou." Sam took Molly gently by the arm and led her to the house. "So does this mean there's no big delivery job waiting for you?"

"Dude, that was Monica…. I mean, Natalie. Not sure how she got my number, but she was waiting for me as I passed by her office. She said a casual hello to me as I walked by, and then she knocked me over the head and shoved me into her car. Nice girl, huh?"

"Really nice. So…you're not leaving?"

"Well, not today, anyway. I will have to go find a delivery soon, and it would be nice to have a full-time gig with a company that places me in regular deliveries up and down the coast."

"If you work fulltime, won't that make it hard to restore your own boat?" *Or go sailing with me?*

"A girl's gotta do what a girl's gotta do. Anyway, *Hullaballoo's* restoration is underway—it's just going to take a long time. I need to be able to make the monthly yard bills, though. Deliveries would be better than waiting tables, you know?" She kissed him on the cheek. "Come on; I'll tell you more about some of the companies I've thought about contacting. Maybe one day, you could deliver a boat with me. Wouldn't that be a blast?"

"Please, no more talk about blasting." Sam pulled her close and kissed her again. "Glad you're okay."

"Better than okay."

CHAPTER TWENTY-NINE

After dinner, Lou insisted on going to see the cannery site herself. With Sam behind the wheel of her car, she chattered away about the day's excitement like a schoolgirl, recounting every second just as she had done for James Bradley upon his arrival and Sam and Molly during their meal.

But when Sam turned into the cannery's driveway, the sight of twisted, melted metal skeleton steel beams made her stop mid-sentence. Sam parked a safe distance away from the building's remains. Neither he nor Molly said a word.

After taking it in, Lou let out a long sigh. "I had such high hopes for this place. Not for myself, mind you, but for Gus and his friends."

"It can still happen, Lou," Molly said quietly from the backseat.

"I don't know, dear. It's such a mess. They would have to start from scratch."

"Bet they are up to the task," Sam said. Looking in the rearview mirror, he perked up. "Look; here comes Gus." The three got out to greet Gus and one of his pals as they pulled up in Gus' battered pickup truck beside Lou's car.

"Evening," Gus called. "We been up here all afternoon, watching the firemen do their best. It's a shame, what happened."

"The biggest shame is that I didn't have time to get the insurance on the property. It's all happened so fast."

"So there's no money to rebuild?" Molly asked the obvious.

"Not a cent from an insurance company," said Lou. "It's just land now. Oh, and a few boats that belong to Lester."

"Does that mean the price is cut?" Gus asked with a smile.

"You could say it's going for fire sale price," Molly said with a laugh. "Sorry; I couldn't help myself."

"Sure," Lou said. "I'll take whatever you want to offer me. I don't want the land, and I don't need the money. In fact, I'll finance the rebuilding of the cannery for you. No banks involved, just the way Harvey would have liked it."

"You a kind woman," Gus said as he gently hugged her.

"And you're a good man. I know you will take good care of this place. Sam, maybe you could consider staying on to help oversee the building and manage the place. It would give you something to do."

"Do I look like I need something to do, Aunt Lou?"

"You're just too young to be retired; that's all."

"I didn't retire; just took a leave of absence."

"He's going to do a bit of traveling, Lou," Molly chimed in.

"Well, that's fine. When he comes back through here, I expect a full report on my grandnephew and then a good visit. Will you be sailing off into the sunset with him, Molly?"

Molly blushed. "Not this trip, Lou. I have some business to finish in Wilmington before I can do that."

"Well, when you finish your work there, you'll have to come back for a visit. My door is always open to you both."

"Thanks, Lou." Molly hugged her. "Gus, want to stop by in the morning? I'll find the paperwork online and we can make this official."

"Yes, that would be fine. I'll go talk to my friends this evening. Bless you, Miss Lou. We will take good care of this place in honor of Mr. Harvey."

"What will you call it?"

"We'll have to sort all that out. Thanks again!" Gus shook hands all around before hopping back into his battered truck to leave.

The beer had warmed by the time Sam took his second swig. Sitting on the front porch, he thought of his options. To stay and help with the rebuilding of the cannery, to go on to Norfolk, or...to head back to Wilmington to help Molly. Was that even an option, or should he let it go? Molly seemed intent on staying on task. She was upstairs packing now. Perhaps he should, too. The provisions list in his lap was woefully short, and Sam didn't have his heart in the task this evening.

Gus would be by in the morning to formalize the cannery land purchase. Once that was done, Molly had no reason to stay. And once she left, Sam had only excuses to put off his trip to Norfolk. On the bright side, Molly said she'd join him after a while, so he had that to look forward to. *Angel* was waiting patiently at anchor, and as of last check, the duck Kathy was nowhere to be seen. Maybe tomorrow would be as good a time as any to leave before the duck found her way back to the boat. Sam knew what he had to do.

CHAPTER THIRTY

Gus was prompt the next morning. His offer of a few thousand dollars was gladly accepted by Lou, and Molly helped formalize the offer. She accompanied the two to Mr. Jackson's office so he could ensure it was legal and then offer advice on how to run the building project. Sam had declined an invitation to go with them, and instead used his car for a grocery run for his voyage north.

When they returned, Lou and Molly celebrated with a mimosa while Sam watched. "A little early, don't you think?"

"Not for a celebration," Molly replied. "Here's to Gus and his friends. May they catch enough fish to sell for many years to come."

"Hear, hear!" Lou raised her glass. "Come on, Sammy; have a little fun with us."

Sam obliged and raised his glass of straight orange juice. "Here's to the new fish market."

"Got anything good to eat?" It was James Bradley, coming in through the back door near the kitchen.

"Of course!" Lou waved him in and offered him a mimosa and an oversized blueberry muffin. James declined the mimosa and accepted a glass of juice from Sam instead.

"To all the good things that have come from the loss of my dear friend, I raise my glass," Lou said.

"And to all the bad that's now accounted for," James added.

"Is it all accounted for?" Sam asked, his glass raised.

"I think so. Paul feels a bit of a fool, I bet. Apparently, Natalie invited her dear friend, the real Miss Maples, up for the charade by saying she wanted to play a little game to see if Paul and the others would recognize Miss Maples as a stranger."

"Well, they do…did look alike," Molly said.

"Yeah, especially when it's dark, and Natalie had encouraged Miss Maples to wear her sailing outfit, including the racing team's shirt. When Paul made his advances, well, I guess Miss Maples was flattered that she'd been able to pull it off."

"Birds of a feather," Lou started to say softly.

"Too bad the game had to end the way it did for her."

"Yeah, Natalie was going to tie it all up in one big, fiery package, wasn't she?" Molly offered.

"That was her intention. I'm glad you're all safe, though." James changed the subject when Sam and Molly made their excuses and walked to the front porch.

"I'm glad you're safe, too," Sam said to Molly. "Stay that way, okay?"

"No prob, Dude. Seems I'm only in trouble when I hang out with you."

"I know."

"Maybe it's just fate?"

"What?"

"Trouble seems to find you no matter where you go, Sam McClellan. The good news…" she hesitated, "is that I will, too."

"Please do." Sam hugged Molly tightly for a full minute before letting go. Picking up her bags, he walked her to the car and helped her in. Not that she needed help. Really.

Standing in the driveway, Sam watched as Molly drove away again in his Mustang.

THE END

Preview of the Next Sam McClellan tale:

HACKED

"You don't understand, Dad," Frank moaned, his head in his hands. Sitting there on the edge of his brown leather couch, his son didn't look like the same man Sam had seen earlier with his mates. Earlier in the day, Frank was filled with bravado, strutting around the office like nothing could touch him. But now, he reminded Sam more of the small boy who lost his favorite red tractor to the tide that one summer so long ago.

"I can't help you if you don't tell me what's going on," Sam said. Hesitating only for a second, Sam sat down on the couch beside Frank. "Look; I know it's been a while since we've seen each other, but nothing's changed. Just tell me what's going on."

Frank rubbed his eyes with the palms of his hands. "Somebody hacked into the cyber security center last night." Frank looked at his father.

Sam felt sure Frank saw the confusion he felt in his face. "You're stepping into an area that I know only a little about."

"This is my life. I'm part of the Criminal Investigative Service for the Coast Guard. It's my job to find gaps in infrastructure so I can support investigations into criminal cyber activity targeting Coast Guard networks. The increase in cyber activity has made it more challenging, but we've been holding our own. Until about six months ago, when we started to see way more activity in international attacks. The hackers could be halfway around the world and still break in, getting vulnerable information."

"We had a cyber team on the police force. I didn't deal with any of that."

"Security is everybody's job these days. Cybercriminals work around the clock to find new ways to get into systems. The Coast Guard is no different—we're a target, just like a big bank would be."

"Okay, so what can I do to help?"

"I'm not sure you can, Dad."

ABOUT THE AUTHOR

North Carolina author Laura S. Wharton writes adventure-suspense and mystery novels for adults, young adults, and children. A careful observer of people and situations around her, Wharton captures readers' imaginations by weaving fact and fiction with a healthy dose of adrenaline into each of her stories.

Award-winning titles include the critically acclaimed adventure, *The Pirate's Bastard,* the tale of the son of a pirate trying to find his place in the New World. Nominated for the prestigious Sir Walter Raleigh Award for Fiction and winner of many more, the story continues to be a favorite of young adults and adults who love a rollicking pirate story.

Also perfect for young adults and adults is the award-winning adventure story *Leaving Lukens,* a coming of age tale of a young girl faced with leaving the only home she's ever known. As World War II encroaches on her small

North Carolina coastal village, she is pulled into a dangerous situation by a sailor who may not be all he appears to be.

Award-winning *In Julia's Garden: A Lily McGuire Mystery* features a snarky landscape architect in Winston-Salem, North Carolina. At the beginning of this contemporary story, Lily McGuire is given a journal that once belonged to a 1940s debutante who vanished. The mystery may be in history, but the journal may also hold clues to the death of Lily's best friend.

Wharton is the author of four mysteries for children, including *Mystery at the Phoenix Festival,* and the popular, award-winning series, *Mystery at the Lake House #1: Monsters Below,* and *Mystery at the Lake House #2: The Mermaid's Tale,* and *The Wizard's Quest.* All of Laura's books involve adventure, fun, a little history, and sailboats. (Laura is a recovering sailor who could backslide at any moment!) Laura Wharton lives in the Triad region of North Carolina, with her husband and son.

Learn more about Laura and her books
at www.LauraWhartonBooks.com.

ACKNOWLEDGMENTS

I hope you have enjoyed reading this book as much as I enjoyed writing it. The *Sam McClellan Tales* are so much fun to write—it's amazing what kind of trouble the characters can find in each story.

I want to thank my most excellent editor, Tyler Tichelaar, and superb cover and book interior design team at Fusion Creative Works.

To longtime friends Claudia and Bodo Brathe, who have graciously and frequently opened their home in Edenton, North Carolina, I say thank you. Their hospitality and knowledge of what has often been hailed as the "prettiest town in the South" helped to form parts of this work of fiction. Their home on Oak Street was the model for Aunt Lou's house, and I will always remember the fun times and pleasant conversations we've had on that gracious front porch.

To my friends (you know who you are) and family who continue to encourage me in my pursuit of this *lovely form of lying* known as fiction, I say a special thank you. It is because you offer an ear and a kind word that I continue to put these stories on paper. To Teddy Clemmons, for the advice on which gun would be best for a certain character in this story, I say thank you.

Thanks, too, to my husband, Bayley, and son, Will, for their patience with me and willingness to pitch in around the house when I'm working on a novel: housekeeping, cooking, and laundry definitely take a backseat to the action between the pages.

No story would be complete without saying a huge thank you to my parents, who have always shared with me their love of the English language. Growing up in a house full of music, love, and laughter, I quickly learned the value of a good story, a snappy comment, and the proper timing for a well-crafted punch line to a joke. May the fun stories never end!

And to my readers who continue to buy my books, write reviews, and tell friends about my stories, I offer my heartfelt thanks. Without such a devoted audience, there wouldn't be a reason for putting the time and effort required into this business. Truly, thank you for your support.

– Laura S. Wharton, 2016

Enjoy These Other Full-Length Novels By

LAURA S. WHARTON

Award-winning Adventures and Mysteries for Adults:

Deceived: A Sam McClellan Tale
In Julia's Garden, A Lily McGuire Mystery
The Pirate's Bastard*
Leaving Lukens*

*Suitable for Young Adults as well.

Award-winning Mysteries for Children:

Mystery at the Lake House #1: Monsters Below
Mystery at the Lake House #2: The Mermaid's Tale
Mystery at the Phoenix Festival
The Wizard's Quest (Early Reader)
Blossom the Possum Learns to Swim (Early Reader)
(by William L. B. Wharton/Illustrations by Laura S. Wharton)

All titles are available as print and e-books.
To learn more about Laura's books,
visit www.LauraWhartonBooks.com

CPSIA information can be obtained
at www.ICGtesting.com
Printed in the USA
FSOW01n0527280416
19769FS

9 780990 466260